CW01033968

Bully Me

Willow Heights Preparatory Academy: The Elite

Book One

selena

Bully Me
Copyright © 2020 selena

Unabridged First Edition
All rights reserved. No part of this book may be reproduced or
transmitted in any form or by any means, electronic or mechanical,
including photocopying, recording, or by any information storage and
retrieval system, without the express written permission of the publisher,
except in cases of a reviewer quoting brief passages in a review.
This book is a work of fiction. Names, characters, places, and
incidents are used factiously. Any resemblance to actual persons, living or
dead, business establishments, and events are entirely coincidental. Use
of any copyrighted, trademarked, or brand names in this work of fiction
does not imply endorsement of that brand.
Published in the United States by Selena and Speak Now.

ISBN-13: 978-1-955913-06-5
Cover © Jodielock Design

For the muse.

Battle not with monsters, lest ye become a monster. And if you gaze into the abyss, the abyss gazes also into you.

—Friedrich Nietzsche

one

My name is Crystal Dolce, and I am anything but sweet. My last name might tell you otherwise, but anyone who knows me also knows the truth. The halls of my school know what I did, but they're afraid to confront me. My parents know what I did, but they excuse it because, let's face it, their reputation is hardly spotless. Around here, what I did is par for the course. Small potatoes.

But not to me.

Someone taps on my door, and I slam my laptop and grab my Gucci bag, ready for school. Royal sticks his head in. "Dad wants to talk to us," he says, giving me a once-over and nodding his approval at my perfectly polished appearance.

"Us?" I ask. "Now? About what?"

My brother shrugs. "I don't know. Let's find out."

"We'll be late."

"Dad probably doesn't even remember that we're in school," Royal points out as we make our way down the hall of our swanky brownstone.

"Probably," I admit, a knot of unease settling in my belly as I enter the kitchen.

"Where are the twins?" Daddy asks, looking up from his laptop.

My oldest brother King is already at the table, a cup of coffee in one hand and a bagel in the other.

"Coming," Duke yells. He and Baron come thundering into the room, shoving to get through the door first.

"Sit down," Daddy says. "I have some news, and I might as well tell you when you're all together."

"Where's Mom?" I ask, as if she's ever up this early. If her weekdays are anything like the weekends, Mom prefers to take her breakfast in bed just before noon, chasing it down with a few cocktails and the pills for all her supposed ills.

"Your mother is sleeping," Daddy says.

"What is it, then?" King asks, getting up to drop a couple bagels into the toaster. "We've got to get to school."

Daddy lays his hands flat on the table and looks from one of us to the next before his announcement. "We're moving."

The air seems to leave the room. For a minute, no one moves. Royal stands halfway in the refrigerator, reaching for the cream cheese. Baron's mouth drops open. Duke just blinks. King turns from the counter to stare at our father. I just sit there, too stunned to speak. At last, the toast pops up, and we all jump.

"What do you mean, moving?" King asks, tossing the bagels onto a plate. "Like, to the *suburbs?*"

"We can't leave the city," Baron says matter-of-factly. "Manhattan is where everything happens."

That doesn't even begin to cover it. Manhattan is our *lives*. And despite the shit that went down last spring, I never imagined leaving our school, let alone New York.

"Not to the suburbs," Daddy says. "To Arkansas."

"To what-the-what?" I ask.

"Like, the state?" Duke asks.

"No, dumbass, the country," Baron says, grabbing the cream cheese and slathering a bagel half.

"Arkansas," King says flatly. His voice sounds about as excited as I feel. I can't think of a place less New York than freaking *Arkansas*. I couldn't find that state on a map if my life depended on it.

"I lived there for a while when I was a kid," Daddy says. "And now I have a business opportunity."

"What kind of business opportunity is in Arkansas?" King asks.

"The kind that's too good to pass up."

"Are you in trouble, Daddy?" I ask, lowering my voice to a whisper. "Do you owe money to… Y'know. The *families?*"

"Don't be dramatic, Crystal," he says. "I think we could all benefit from the change."

People always whisper about the mafia, and I know my father's name gets thrown in there, but that's because he's a successful, Italian-American businessman who started from nothing over in the Bronx. Not Arkansas. I've never heard of any childhood in the south. Dad has a Bronx accent, for god's sake.

"Where in Arkansas?" King asks. I can see the wheels already turning in his head as he weighs the possibilities, the pros and cons, and how he can make this move easier on all of us. All my brothers are protective, but he's the heart of us.

"Faulkner," Daddy says. "It's a small town. Think of it as… An opportunity."

"An opportunity to live in a shitty little town in the south?" Royal asks with a scowl.

"An opportunity to be a big fish in a small pond."

"We're already big fish," Duke points out.

"In a big pond," Baron adds.

"Daddy, why are you doing this to us?" I blurt out. "Is this because of what happened with me and Veronica?"

Daddy's jaw tightens, and he snaps his laptop closed. "Considering the trouble you've all gotten into lately, I'd think you'd be happy for a fresh start. Maybe you can think about what kind of start you want to make it."

He gets up, sweeps his laptop off the table, and strides out of the room, leaving us standing there with uneaten bagels, looking at anything but each other. I wonder if a little thrill of possibility is running through my brothers, too.

two

A new start. How many people dream of it, and how few get it. A chance to start over, to leave your past behind. But also… Your present. This morning my father informed me we're leaving the only home I've ever known. My school. My friends. My life.

My mistakes.

Everything, gone.

For the rest of the day, I walk around in a daze.

At noon, I ditch and go home, crawling into bed to write a blog post before Mom's up to ask questions. Not that she'll notice if I'm home. It's only a month into sophomore year, and I've already skipped too many days. So far, my parents haven't said anything, though. I'm pretty sure my brothers are intercepting the mail, and my parents aren't really interested in my academics. But Mom will be pissed if I make her look bad, if it looks like she doesn't know what her daughter's up to. The other moms might talk about her behind her back, and we can't have that. We're Dolces, after all.

I hear my brothers get home, but when Royal sticks his head in my room, I pretend to be sleeping. I can't deal with one more thing just now. Daddy's words ring in my head, circling back on themselves, repeating over and over.

A new start.

We can choose who we want to be. What kind of people would we be in a small town in the south? Is this punishment? Or penance? Can I pay for my sins somewhere far from the scene of the crime?

I hear Dad get home, and I know when he tells Mom because her blood-curdling scream echoes through the brownstone. Mom *is* New York. Without Tiffany's, Barney's, and Bloomingdale's; without her Manhattan Moms clubs, galas, and cocktails on yachts with backstabbing socialites, Mom wouldn't know what to do with herself.

SELENA

I cram my earbuds in and sink down in my bed, pulling my laptop into my lap and diving down the rabbit hole of online shoe shopping. The crash of a plate hitting the wall downstairs startles me out of my gluttony, and I yank out an earbud. Mom's shriek of rage pierces my eardrums through the floor.

I could've escaped the house before the battle started like my brothers. They offered to let me go with them, but partying with my brothers is the very opposite of fun. They hover over me at parties, watching my drinks and intimidating any guy who talks to me. And it's not like I can sneak out to a party without them. Someone will call them the second I show up. They rule our school, and that means no one wants to piss them off by helping me do something they don't think befits a Dolce daughter.

The only reason my brothers offered is because they think if they take me out, I can forget what's happening to our family. The problem is, they won't let me do any of the things they do to forget. I don't get to drink or hook up or start fights. I'm a Dolce girl. I have to behave.

BULLY ME

"I'm tired of being your mafia wife," Mom shrieks downstairs. I cram my earbuds back in and hit the volume button until Sia is all I hear. At last, the house goes quiet, and I drag myself out of bed and sink into a hot bath. I can't stop thinking about the silence in the house, and how pretty soon my parents will be making a different kind of noise. Gross as it is, my parents are probably about to fuck. After they blow up at each other, they usually make up in as spectacular a fashion as they fight. Probably how they ended up with five kids. Tonight, though, the brownstone remains eerily silent.

Everything is changing.

"Crystal, sweetheart. Are you in here?" Mom trills from my room, sounding so bright and chipper I know she must have taken some extra happy pills with her evening cocktails.

"In the bath," I call.

And because my family doesn't know about a little thing called boundaries, Mom comes waltzing into my *ensuite* bathroom.

"There you are," she says. "I've been looking all over for you." She sinks onto my makeup stool, adjusting her flowing red dress with her free hand while holding her martini aloft with the other.

"I've been in my room the whole time," I point out, rearranging a pile of bubbles since Mom has been known to critique my body without invitation. She doesn't seem to realize that movie star elegance doesn't necessarily pass down through the genes. I'm lucky I got enough of her beauty—her thick, chestnut waves and ink-dark eyes—to be admitted to the popular circle at school. I always see my beauty as somehow superficial, though, as if it can be stolen at any moment. I try too hard, care too much. Mom carries hers inside her. It's effortless. She is Old Hollywood Glamour. I am... Not.

"Your father tells me he's already given you the news," she says.

"Yeah," I say, pushing myself up against the end of the deep, clawfoot tub. "We're moving."

"Yes," she says, looking thoughtful as she sips her martini. "I suppose you are."

My heart does a funny little skipping, twisting thing inside me. "You're not going."

"Don't look so shocked, dear," she says. "You know I can't simply pick up my life and move it to Alabama. I'm a Manhattan girl."

"Arkansas."

She waves a dismissive hand. "Wherever."

"So… What? You and Daddy are getting a divorce?"

"We didn't get to that," she says. "I had to get ready to go out. There's a fundraiser at the MET tonight."

"You're just leaving Daddy in the middle of a fight to go hang out with some people you barely know and don't even like?"

Typical Mom, but still.

"Don't make it sound so dramatic," she says. "It's really not. It's simple. He's moving across the country. I'm not."

"So it is divorce."

"As you can see, I'm not the bad guy here, Crystal. I'm just going on with my life as I have. He's the one making changes, making big demands."

That's what was on my mind all day. If I could stay, somehow, would I? Or is Daddy right? Maybe a chance to start over isn't the worst thing in the world.

Maybe going on with our lives as we have is.

"Do we have to choose?" I ask. "You or Daddy?"

Mom sighs dramatically and sets down her empty glass on my makeup counter. "Your father and I have been fighting for years. It was only a matter of time. I never thought we'd still be together when you children started high school, let alone when you were nearly ready for college."

"I thought that's just how you were," I say. "How you liked it."

Now that I said it out loud, it sounds all kinds of fucked up. Just because all I've ever known is their fighting and making up, that doesn't mean love is supposed to be that way.

"I think I'd just like some time alone," Mom says, standing with a grace she somehow maintains even after countless martinis. "I don't even know who I am without all of you. What do *I* want? Without your father, without you kids to think about, what would I do with myself? Who am I?"

"Is this really the best moment for your latest existential crisis?" I ask, crossing my arms over my chest.

"How many times have you gone out for ice cream this month?" Mom asks, eyeing the ample swell of my breasts.

"Mom!"

"To have such perky ones again," she says with another sigh. "Oh, well. I'd better get going, or I'll be late to dinner."

When she leaves, I slide down under the bubbles and lay on the bottom of the tub, holding my breath and staring up through the water.

I heard drowning doesn't hurt, I said to Veronica as we floated on top of the pool this summer. *Do you think it's true?*

"Why do you think about that stuff?" she snapped. *"That's so morbid, Crystal. You really need to stop."*

And I wanted to remind her of the time I'd told her we needed to stop, and she hadn't listened. But I didn't say anything because I thought, what if I wasn't her best friend? I know how quickly fortunes turn.

I hear my phone chime outside the bathtub, but I lie there longer, seeing how long I can hold my breath. I wonder how fast it would be. Could I open my mouth and take one big gulp, and that would be the end? I imagine water rushing into my lungs, filling them like water balloons.

I sit up straight, sucking in a giant gulp of air. My lungs are burning. It doesn't seem possible that drowning can be painless if even imagining it hurts. I grab a towel and jump out of the tub as if the water might pull me under, suck me down the drain.

My phone screen flashes a new text from King asking if everything is okay here. He might be out partying, but his mind is here with me as I watch our family implode. Of course it is. Our family means more to him than anyone, even our parents.

I slump onto my stool and think of what to say. Something that will let them know Mom's decision but reassure them that I'm fine with it. Something that doesn't sound like I'm whining about being rejected by my mommy. After all, she rejected them, too. My heart squeezes for them. I know how much they love the city. I might want a chance to start over, but they have no reason to. They didn't fuck up their lives.

At least we'll all be together. That's a consolation. They'll be right by my side, conquering the halls of our new school the same way they did our old one.

And me?

Maybe I don't want that anymore. I did all that, and look where it got me. I'm exhausted, used up, broken. It took too much effort to claw my way to the top and stay there. Once I got there, it hardly seemed worth it. There's only one way to go when you get to the top.

This time, I get to choose. I don't have to do it all again. No one in Arkansas will know who I am. I can be anyone. I could even choose to be no one at all. I've done the whole Queen B thing, the Dolce Princess thing. Maybe, like Daddy said, it's time for a change.

three

Running away from our problems is a favorite family tradition, but this is the first time we've done it literally. Usually we float away on a numb cloud of bliss, watching a tequila sunrise after a night of valium oblivion. We fly around the world chasing the next opportunity, so we don't have to look at the ones we've missed while standing in our own living room. But today, we ran.

I didn't look back.

"Oh my god, what is this? I thought summer was over," I moan as sweat breaks out on my face the instant we step off Daddy's plane.

He spreads his arms wide and grins, his mirrored sunglasses reflecting back my own miserable image.

"Welcome to September in the South," he says. "We call this Indian summer."

"First off, I'm pretty sure that's an offensive term," I say. "Secondly, what's with all this 'we' talk. You're from the Bronx, Daddy."

"We make strong associations with the place we spend our formative years," Royal murmurs behind me. "Dad's obviously got some attachment to this place."

I don't see much to attach oneself to. The town is flat as a freaking pancake and so hot it makes me feel like an ant under some psycho god's microscope.

"Where are all the buildings?" I ask. "Where are the people?"

"It's a small town," Daddy says. "Don't worry. You'll do great here. You'll be a novelty at your new school. Everyone will want to make friends with you. And once they see how talented you are, making the team will be a piece of cake."

"This one time, he might be right," Royal says, taking my bag and leading me to the Cayenne waiting to take us to the new house Daddy bought. Apparently he's been coming down here on business for a few months, and last week, he came down to get the house and cars settled. Now it's real. We own a house here. We live here. Permanently.

It's too surreal to comprehend. I'm a bundle of nerves, giddiness at the prospect of starting over mixed with the familiar fear that nibbled at my insides for the past six months. A blast of hot wind sweeps across the flat concrete lot outside the hangar, dust pelting my bare legs.

"This town is a joke," Duke says, diving into the welcoming air-conditioned interior of the car. "We'll own this school in two seconds flat." He throws an arm around me as Royal slides in on my other side. Dad sits up front and directs the driver. King and Baron decided to road trip the move, mostly because they didn't believe they could find the kind of cars they like in Arkansas. After seeing this town from the air, I have no doubt they're correct.

"Please tell me that's not our school," I say, covering my eyes as we drive by a tan building with narrow windows that looks like a prison.

Duke laughs and gives my shoulders a squeeze. "That's the public school. Look how sad it looks."

I peek out from between my fingers and see a statue of a weird six-legged cat creature. A blonde couple stands against its base, making out while their friends talk and laugh around them.

A funny ache curls up under my sternum, and I tear my eyes away.

"Breathe," I whisper, closing my eyes and laying my head back against the cool leather. My brothers are right. Daddy's right. We'll be fine here. We'll go to the good school across town, not the one where trashy people make out in public for all the world to see. We'll be fine. More than fine.

Royal gives my knee a quick squeeze, then twists around, watching the school until it disappears from sight.

"The only thing good about Faulkner High is the football program," Daddy says from the front seat. "Believe it or not, they're a big rival of Willow Heights."

Willow Heights. Our new school. Dad came back from buying the house here with flyers about Willow Heights Preparatory Academy, application forms that his secretary filled out while he laughed about the 'high tuition,' which is peanuts compared to our old school. He made up the difference with a generous donation, which he promised would make us royalty with the admin the moment we walked in the door. It's up to us to make sure we're royalty with the students.

If we want to be.

*

We pull up to a gate a few minutes later. At last, something looks promising. The drive through town was downright depressing. The tallest building in the entire town is maybe three stories. Everything is weirdly slow, as if it's sluggish from the heat. Besides a few fast food places, gas stations, and something that apparently passes as a mall, there's not much going on in Faulkner.

But as we enter our gated community, sprawling green lawns stretch before us. Huge shade trees dominate the yards, and behind them stand enormous houses that belong in an old movie.

"Welcome home," Daddy says, spreading out his arms toward the entire neighborhood before twisting around to check our reactions.

His words have me swallowing hard, half terrified that I've just stepped into a world I know nothing about and half giddy with excitement at the unfathomable difference between this and our Manhattan brownstone. We have a vacation house in the Virgin Islands, but this is...

Our new home.

The car slows, and I stare down a long walkway that leads under the gently arching branches of two rows of mossy trees bending over it as if they're bowing to the royalty that walks beneath. The walkway cuts through the lush, green, perfectly cut lawn to the front of an enormous white plantation-style home with rows of towering white columns, black window trim, and an intricate black railing on the balcony that stretches along the entire second floor.

As I'm gaping at the house, about to ask Daddy if it's ours, a classic convertible shoots by us on the right side, spitting gravel at the Porsche like we're a taxi in the wrong lane. I catch a flash of blond hair and a masculine profile before it swerves back onto the road inches in front of us, shoots forward, and skids into the driveway of the house. The car roars down the drive and disappears behind the house.

I bite my lip and glance up at Daddy, but he doesn't even flinch, let alone take off after the asshole driver. Instead, he laughs.

"I better not catch any of you driving like that knucklehead," he says, gesturing to the next house. The driver pulls in as I turn to Royal, widening my eyes.

"Knucklehead?" I mouth incredulously.

Daddy has never used that word in his life. He's notorious for swearing nastily and vehemently. It's like we've suddenly stepped back into the 1950s. Even the convertible was reminiscent of an older time, all spiffed out and in mint condition.

Our driver pulls into the driveway Daddy indicated. This house does not have a row of trees for the front walkway, but it has the same sprawling lawn, huge shade trees, and meticulous landscaping. An enormous white plantation house sits back from the road, with two curving staircases leading up to the second-floor balcony like a pair of welcoming arms.

Daddy turns to us and grins. "I thought you might like to have a little freedom to come and go as you please."

"Wow," I say, because I'm not sure what else to say. I feel like I just stepped onto the set of *Gone With the Wind*.

"Not you," Daddy says. "The boys. You'll keep an eye on your baby sister, right?"

Royal salutes him. "That's what brothers are for. To do the job dads are supposed to do."

Daddy ignores his little dig and hops out of the car when it stops. He opens our door and gestures toward the house with a flourish. "Welcome to the new Dolce family home."

four

Who would you be if you could be anyone? I'm not sure I know. I never got to choose before, and I don't know if I do now. Sometimes, I think my whole life was manufactured by my family.

Here's what I'd choose. I want to be… Better.

Not better than everyone else. Better than me. Better than I was. But I don't know if that's asking for too much. My family expects me to be better than everyone else, just like they are.

I lie in bed the night before our first day of school, listening to the big house settling around us. Daddy's still at the office, working late to get everything in order for the new branch he's opening here. I can't seem to sleep in the new, strange house. Foreign noises invade my consciousness—the crickets and other insects so loud I can hardly go outside after dark, the wind through trees making eerie sighs like restless ghosts in the hot night.

Tonight, another sound that I can't identify rouses me from my half-sleep. I check my phone. It's midnight, and Daddy's car still hasn't turned into the white gravel drive. Outside, an irregular slapping sound catches my attention. I snag a silk robe from the back of my closet door and step outside, cinching it around my waist. A gust of hot wind sweeps over me, and I think I must have heard a loose shutter banging somewhere.

Twack!

The sound is somehow familiar, though I can't tell what it is. I peer down into the bright moonlight that lights up the entire yard in an eerie glow. The balcony runs all the way around the top floor of the house, though my room is on the far back corner. To reach the stairs, I'd have to walk past Duke's windows on one side and then King's windows on two sides since he has the front corner room. I'm pretty sure they set it up that way on purpose.

From the balcony outside my room, I can see the back yard, the side yard, and the row of lilac bushes that forms the boundary between the houses. According to the new housekeeper who came with the house, they're quite impressive in springtime. Beyond the lilacs, a slice of the neighbor's backyard and one side of their house are visible. A handful of looming shade trees toss in the heat and wind as I wait for the sound that disturbed my attempted slumber.

Suddenly, something small and dark races between the lilacs and into the moonlit yard. I gasp, startled into thinking it's a varmint for a second. But then it rolls to a stop in the dewy grass, and I see that it's something much more familiar than a yard pest. A football.

I blink at it, not sure if I'm dreaming. The light on the dew gives everything a silvery, dreamlike quality. Then a tall, blond guy steps between the lilacs. He's wearing nothing but a pair of drawstring sweats hanging so low on his hips that I can see more of him than I should want to. His body is slicked in sweat, his tan skin glistening in the moonlight. I swallow, my eyes raking from his tattooed shoulders, over his washboard abs, down to the V of muscle that dips into the waistband of his pale grey sweats, which he's cut off at the knee.

It's not like I've never seen a guy in nothing but shorts before. My brothers spend half their time dressed that way. But this boy is not my brother. He's thinner than my brothers, less bulky, but every bit as muscular in a more lean, ropy way. The kind of muscle you might get from working instead of working out. His skin is more golden than the olive tone my Italian brothers have, and his tan is concentrated on his shoulders and arms, like he got it from being outside. I can see so much of him, and yet, seeing doesn't illuminate. Each thing I notice is a mystery, a question instead of an answer.

He trots across our lawn, picks up the ball, and draws back like he's going to throw a long, spiral pass toward his house. Just before he completes the pass, he hesitates. Lowering the ball, he turns slowly. My body freezes, but my heart races. Every part of me knows that I should duck back into the shadows on the balcony, that I shouldn't let the careless-driving, football-tossing insomniac neighbor see me watching him.

And yet.

For one reckless moment, I want something other than what is. I don't want to be Crystal Dolce, darling daughter of a possible mob family and coddled sister of four very dangerous boys. I don't want to be the mean girl who did a terrible thing, or the one who's off limits to every boy if they want to live. I don't want to be the Queen B or cheerleader.

I want to be seen. I want to be a girl standing in my silk robe in the moonlight, with my disheveled hair streaming in the hot midnight wind and the moon making me luminous. I want to be a mystery to him, too. I want him to see me and want to solve this mystery.

His eyes settle on mine, and he stills. For a long moment, no one moves. The see-saw music of the crickets falls away. The shimmering moonlight disappears. The suffocating heat of the night dissipates, and the wind dies. There is only us, suspended in time, in place. I sink into the ocean depths of his eyes, plunging deeper and deeper below the surface until nothing else exists.

The crunch of tires on gravel invades our world, the one we built for only us. Headlights sweep across the front of our house, and I glance that way to see Daddy's car pulling into the drive. When I turn back, the boy is gone, leaving me to wonder if I dreamed the moment with him.

*

"Crys, what are you doing?" King asks, banging on my bathroom door.

"I'm changing my tampon, what do you think?" I yell, shoving my phone into my pocket.

"Let's go," he says. "It's time."

"Time to dominate," Duke yells, thudding a fist against my door.

I take one last look at myself in the mirror. For a minute, I considered changing my image. But I've been this person so long, I don't know what else to be. Maybe it's who I really am. Pretty. Spoiled.

Mean.

At any rate, I look the same as I've always looked. I don't dare change my image. I thought, for a minute, I might be a girl who wore slouchy sweats, oversized T's, and messy buns. But my brothers wouldn't let me out of the house like that. We have an image to uphold. Dolces take care of themselves and each other. Looking the part is half the battle.

SELENA

I run a brush through my dark locks, straightened to perfection after an hour of work. Collecting my hair into a long, low pony, I drape it forward over one shoulder. After smoothing on a thin layer of product to enhance the shine and tame flyaways, I head out of my bathroom.

My brothers step back and look me over. They've all gathered outside my door wearing slacks and buttoned shirts to fit the dress code. I feel bad for them having to wear pants and long-sleeved shirts in this heat.

"Is that lipstick too dark?" King asks.

"It's what I always wear," I tell him, making a kissy-face. "My signature."

"Is that skirt shorter than your uniform at our old school?" he asks, eyeing my hemline.

I'm excited to be able to wear real clothes here, since Willow Heights has a strict dress code but no uniform. "Stop looking at my legs, perv," I say, pushing past them and out of my bedroom.

By some silent agreement, we all climb into Royal's new Range Rover, a "gift" from Daddy that was more like a bribe to come here without making a fuss. I'd expected them to each take their own car to show off, but maybe my brothers are as nervous as I am.

They'd never show it, though.

"Look at this pathetic little town," Duke says as we pull out of our opulent neighborhood and start toward the school. "We're going to rule this school the second we step through the doors."

"Not me," I say, my voice sounding light though I was too nervous to even think about breakfast. If I've learned anything in the past year, it's that power can be a dangerous thing. I don't want to rule anymore, and I told my brothers as much. They don't get it, but they're trying to be understanding. They've never wanted to be normal. They love the power.

I have to admit, I loved it, too. I loved it until the moment I saw what it could do. Until the moment I lost control of it. But here? No one knows me. I could be normal. Have a friend who didn't know the worst things about me, our shared guilt hanging between us like a noose. Maybe I could even have a boyfriend, someone my brothers actually liked instead of one they allowed to escort me to some function and then promptly dismissed like a servant.

Things will be better here, like Daddy promised. A new start is just what we all need.

We pull into the parking lot, and my chest tightens, my resolve crumbling. How easy it would be to march down the hall like I put the *B* in *Queen B*. I've been that girl so long, it's my default. But no more. Here, I'll be different. Better.

"Ready, Crystal?" Royal asks.

"What if I'm not?" I whisper, meeting his pure cacao eyes when he twists around in his seat.

"Relax, would you?" Baron asks, shoving my shoulder. "This school is a joke. One day here, and everyone will be eating out of our hands."

"Or licking our shoes," King says, glancing at us in the rearview mirror.

"I got something else the hot ones can lick," Duke says, grabbing himself for emphasis.

King pulls into a parking spot at the back of the lot, halfway under the shade of a towering oak. I know he's doing it for me, parking back here so we can talk without prying eyes checking out the new guys. Otherwise, my brothers would be parking front and center, soaking up the attention. They're not exactly the slip-in-unnoticed type. They couldn't be if they tried, so they don't bother trying.

"I guarantee you, anything this tiny town has going on can't even touch what goes on in our old school," King says, turning to pat my knee. "We're gonna take this place by storm in a matter of minutes, and you know why?"

"Because we're the Dolces," I mutter.

"Yeah we are," Duke and Baron yelled in unison, pumping their fists in the air. They're identical, but they've taken great pains to distinguish themselves at this school. Baron even wears a pair of glasses instead of his usual contacts, and Duke got his hair cut short, forsaking their usual tousled look.

"Let's go kick ass," King says.

I know they've reached their limits in dealing with my anxiety, so I take a deep breath and center myself by meeting Royal's eyes again. He's the quietest of my brothers, my twin, the one who can always calm me down when I start to lose it.

SELENA

We climb out of the Range Rover, and I straighten my skirt and smooth my hair as we get into formation. King is the center of our family, the center of our group. Royal and I step up beside him, and my younger brothers each fall in at opposite ends, the first line of defense. I don't know when we created this formation, but it's as predictable as a football formation on the field. We're ready. With a nod, King sets the play in motion, and we start across the lot.

"Thank the baby Jesus the girls here aren't ugly," Duke says as we pass a group of girls primping next to a pickup truck. They stop to gawk, and Duke shoots them an inviting smile.

My brothers are, to put it mildly, noticeable. They're all over six feet and built like the athletes they are. To add to that, they all inherited our parents' good looks—in spades.

We make it toward the front of the lot, the primo parking spaces designated for the students who want to pay for a spot, each with a big yellow number painted on the asphalt. There, I spot the long, sleek, powder-blue classic convertible that cut us off the day we moved in.

Our neighbor. Considering where they live, it's no surprise that they have the best spot in the entire lot, right next to the walkway that leads to the door of Willow Heights Prep. They probably paid through the nose for that. Suddenly, I'm glad we parked at the back. We can scout out the school this way. It's always good to know the ones to watch, even if you're planning to become the ones to watch.

Three guys stand leaning against the car as if waiting for us. I scan their faces, trying to recognize the boy I saw last night. A blond guy with strong, angular features leans casually against the rear of the car, one foot on the ground and the other propped on the bumper, his hands resting on the edge of the trunk.

Not him.

Beside him, standing straight and tall right behind the car, stands a taller, more muscular version of the same guy, his square, broad shoulders commanding even from a distance. His sleeves are rolled up, revealing a tattoo on golden-tanned forearms, which are currently crossed over a broad chest. He glares at us, his blue eyes icy cold.

A swarm of butterflies explodes inside me. *Him.*

SELENA

Oh, fuck. Definitely him.

On his other side, another blond slouches against the trunk of the car, leaning back on it with his elbows while he scrolls through his phone, paying us no mind.

I have plenty of time to take them in before we arrive at the front of the lot. I bring my attention back to our insomniac neighbor, the angry-looking guy. He's the driver, the center, just as King is ours. And he doesn't look like he's here to throw us a welcome party. I glance sideways at King, wondering how we're going to play this. If he'll speak first, if he'll make nice.

"Parking back in the nosebleed with the scholarship kids?" the glaring guy drawls in a smooth, silky voice that sends a little shock of electricity through me. I didn't expect that. I didn't expect that gorgeous voice, like warm honey melting over my bare skin. And I didn't expect what my body did when I heard it.

"Someone's in our spot," King says, nodding to the Bel Air. For a second, no one speaks. The guy on his phone lifts his head, shaking a fringe of shiny blond hair from his eyes. A few people have gathered around, curious about the new kids and ready for a showdown.

"You think this is your spot?" the angry guy asks. He's good-looking, with a sculpted jawline and a square chin with the hint of a dimple in the center, but his eyes are hard and mean. The guy on his left has sharper features, a pointed chin and a sharp nose along with bright, curious blue eyes, but I peg them as brothers.

"It will be tomorrow," King says, and he keeps walking, so we keep walking.

We stride up the set of wide, shallow steps to the high front doors. The building is a huge brick thing with the entire name of the school—Willow Heights Preparatory Academy—carved into a long slab of marble high above the doors. Just over the entrance is a smaller marble inset bearing the school motto: *Inis Origine Pendet.*

We enter the building and find the office, where we collect our schedules and meet our guides for the day. They're introduced as the student council, a group of pretty, preppy blondes who look like clones with perfectly straight, smooth, long hair and high heels. As we disperse, I notice my guide,

Lacey, gazing after my brothers with longing. Guess she drew the short straw.

"So, what's the deal around here?" I ask.

Lacey strides ahead we make our way down the hall away from the office. "The classes are hard," she says. "So if you're from the ghetto or something, you better expect to spend a lot more time than you probably spent on your classes in Brooklyn."

There is so much wrong with that sentence that I don't even bother to correct her. I have bigger things to worry about and limited time to learn what I need to know.

"I'm not worried about the classes," I say. "Tell me about those guys out front. The blonds in the Bel Air."

"The Darlings," she says without hesitation, as if she was expecting that question.

"Brothers?"

"Cousins," she says. "They're one of Faulkner's founding families. Their great-great-great grandfather of so many generations back settled here in the 1700s or something."

"I'm more interested in the ones that go here now than their ancestry."

She gives me a pitying look. "This is the south, honey. Family means something here."

I already don't like this bitch, but I keep my mouth shut. She doesn't have to tell me about the importance of family. But I need information, not an enemy.

"Got it," I say. "So, they're royalty in this school because of their name."

"They're royalty in this *town*," Lacey corrects. "They get whatever they want. You're new, so one of them will probably want to get in your pants."

"You don't need to worry about that," I say, sensing her resentment in that statement. "I don't date."

"If they want to date you, you'll date," she says. "They get whatever, and whoever, they want. Their family pays the salary of everyone who works at this school. Learn the way things work around here, and you'll be fine."

"Well, thanks," I say. "Guess I'll figure it out soon enough."

Lacey stops at my class, having pointed out the others along the way. "You want my advice?" she asks, planting a hand on her hip. "Say yes to whatever they want, try to keep your dignity when they're done with you, and move on. Don't be fooled into thinking you're special. You won't be the first girl to get screwed by a Darling boy, and you won't be the last. Don't take it personal."

"Even less interested now," I say. "My brothers are protective. They'd never let me date a guy like that, and I wouldn't want to."

"You'd be lucky to land one of them. Devlin doesn't really do the whole dating thing, but the others have a short attention span. If you play your cards right, you could be a Darling Doll. The Dolls are set for their entire time at Willow Heights."

She's obviously into the Darling cousins, and she doesn't care much what I have to say. I'm fine with that. I'm more into listening today. This is a new school, and I don't want to step on the wrong toes and draw attention. I'll have to wait and see what my brothers say, find out the game plan. I might end up being best friends with this girl. At a school like this, it's all about social status, not about deeper connections. If I dated a Darling, I could be in her group. I could have status. I could be a *Darling Doll.*

The name makes me want to gag, but I don't show my distaste. I'm lucky she's laying it out so clearly for me. I'm still not even sure what I want, and if I can have it. I'm not sure I can be a wallflower. It's not the Dolce way. But that doesn't mean I can't be someone different than I was before.

The one thing I know for sure is that I want to be better, to find some way to pay for what I've done. But I don't know how I'm going to do that. I'm okay observing until I figure it out. If helping take down the kings of this school and letting my brothers step into their shoes is going to assuage my guilt, I'll do it. I know that's what my family wants, so I'll probably do it, whether or not it's what I truly want. Sometimes, we all make sacrifices for each other. That's what family is all about.

A soft bell chimes, and students begin to appear at the ends of the hallway, coming in for classes.

"Thanks for showing me around," I say, sliding my schedule into my bag. "I think I've got it for the rest of the day."

"I have one piece of advice for anyone new in town," Lacey says. "Faulkner is built on tradition. We're set in our ways, and we don't like to see those ways disrupted. That goes for your entire family. Don't make waves, and you might survive."

five

The first day at a new school. My one chance to make a first impression. Who will I be? Who would I be if I didn't have to be a Dolce daughter, instructed to take my rightful place in the social hierarchy—at the top? If I had a choice, I might wonder. I don't, so wondering is a waste of time. Dolce's don't dwell on what-ifs. We see what we want, what we deserve, and we take it.

"Hey, girl," drawls a sexy southern voice as I make my way to my next class, typing out an entry on my blog.

I look up to see one of the Darlings, the one with the longish hair swished across his forehead. His voice is almost as sexy as our neighbor's and full of mischief that makes me want to smile back even though I know better.

"Whatever you're going to ask, the answer is no," I say before I can get sucked in by his playful smile that reminds me a little of Duke's. But while Duke is all energy, like a cute puppy, this guy looks like he's biding his sweet time before he decides on a plan of attack. There's something calculated in the way he strolls along, as if the world moves at the pace he sets. I realize too late that I've slowed to his pace, that I've fallen into step with him as if he's drawn me in with the gravity of his very presence.

I won't be a moon orbiting him or any of his cousins. I have my own sun to orbit—King. He's the brightest light, the one that gives life and keeps the worlds turning in the Dolce universe.

"I was just going to say we're in the next class together," he says. "You can't say no to that."

"How do you know what class I have next?"

"Magic," he says with a wink.

"Very funny."

"I like to think I am," he drawls. "I'm also Colt. Colt Darling."

"Of course you are."

He quirks an eyebrow, smiling wider. "So you've heard of me?"

"No, I meant, of course your name is Colt. I bet you wear cowboy boots with your uniform."

"Sometimes," he says, swishing his hair out of his eyes with a toss of his head. He's got that lazy, easy charm, like a teen Matthew McConaughey. "So, you got a name, or should I just call you New York?"

"Crystal Dolce."

"Sweet."

"I assure you, I'm not."

Colt laughs this slow, drawling laugh. "Let's sit together."

"I'm not sure that's a good idea."

He gives me a lazy smile. "I'm funny, remember? I'll make you laugh."

"Can I laugh *at* you?"

"I'll be laughing, too," he says. "Guess you'll have to settle for laughing with me."

"Is that how things work around here?" I ask. "We're either with you, or against you?"

"How else could it work?" he asks, sauntering into the classroom in that slow, easy way of his. My eyes are drawn in, captivated by the confident walk, and the next thing I know, I'm checking out his ass for a second when he's in front of me.

This shit has got to stop. Before it begins.

He sits down at a desk and pats the one beside him.

"Why do I get the feeling I'm going to be taking someone else's seat?" I ask. "I'm sure you don't sit alone."

"They'll deal," he says. "Sit."

I want to disobey, but the thought of sitting alone in a class full of strangers, of enduring their stares and whispers of speculation as I did last period, has me sliding into the seat. It's not like anyone else is going to ask me to sit with them. And as much as I hate to admit it, I'm flattered by his attention. He's adorable, with that playful smile, drawling southern accent, and the swish of golden hair he keeps playing with.

"Good girl," he says, squeezing my knee under the desk. The touch of his hot, calloused hand on my bare knee makes me jump, and I move my leg away, but the sensation is not exactly unpleasant. This is so not good. My brothers have already started shit with this family. Being attracted to any of them is the worst move I could make.

I'm startled by the little thrill that goes through me at the thought of defying them.

I couldn't do that, though. We're the Dolces. We stick together. Nothing in this world is more important than that, and there's not a guy in this world who could come between us. Definitely not this too-charming-for-his-own-good guy who I've already been warned is a player who will take what he wants and leave me to pick up the shreds of my dignity.

I do my best to ignore Colt for the rest of class, a boring English lecture about *Romeo and Juliet*, which I read like ten times at my old school.

"Want me to come to your balcony tonight?" Colt asks halfway through class.

I roll my eyes and put a finger to my lips.

A second later, a piece of paper slides across his desk onto mine. Colt's handwriting is scrawled across it, big messy letters that speak of zero effort. *I hear you live next door to Devlin.*

I write one word and nudge the paper back.

So?

I know where you live. I could come to your window.

We're not Romeo and Juliet.

We could be.

No. We couldn't.

You're right. You're not 13, and I'm not a suicidal perv.

I stifle a laugh. *Idk, saying you know where I live is kinda pervy.*

I'm not sure how I feel about Devlin telling him where I live, or the fact that Devlin has said anything about us at all. In the few days it took us to settle in, they haven't made an effort to come by and welcome us to the neighborhood or anything, but apparently Devlin knew we were there all along.

Colt slides the paper back to me.

Not pervy, just a fact. So how about 10ish? I can throw pebbles.

I shake my head and scribble a few lines back. *Unless you want to die, I suggest you leave my windows alone. I have four very big, very protective brothers. And a father who may or may not be in the mafia.*

I consider leaving off the last line, but it never hurts to have that question in the back of people's minds. We're Italian, so ignorant people like to ask that question anyway. Might as well answer it before they ask. It offers a layer of protection, respect, and fear. We embrace those rumors, neither confirming nor denying. It's part of the Dolce image, part of our mystery.

Colt pushes the paper back, his one line of lazy print taking up three or four lines on the notebook paper.

I'm not scared.

I don't answer that, because too many thoughts are racing through my mind. He should be scared. My brothers don't joke around when it comes to guys messing with me. Even if not for them, I don't want to start up something complicated. I have a lot to atone for, and if I want to be someone new, someone better, it doesn't start like this. It's not an option, anyway, so I push the thought away.

Colt nudges my elbow with his, giving me a pair of puppy dog eyes that would make a weaker woman melt. Okay, fine, it makes me melt. But I'm not falling for it. I can't. I'm not here to fall in love.

I turn to face forward and refuse to look at him again. Only when class ends do I realize that no one came to claim my seat. Either Colt usually sits alone, or his word is unspoken law, and the person who sits there simply accepted that I've displaced them.

After class, I slip out and down the hall before I can do anything stupid. I'm halfway down the hall when I hear a commotion. It sounds like a pack of dogs have gotten into the school, but when I turn the corner, I see a group of students crammed together like they're watching a fight. Except they're all barking. It might be funny if they weren't making the sounds deep in their throats, like something bloodthirsty and primitive.

I hesitate, pretty sure I do not want to know what's happening. But my feet carry me forward, and the next thing I know, I'm hurrying along the hall, shouldering my way through the crowd to see what the fuss is all about. Shoving my way past a Darling cousin with a hysterically giggling Lacey on his arm, I reach the center of the circle.

My first glimpse shows me Devlin Darling standing with his back against the lockers, holding a sobbing girl by the back of her neck. Everyone crowds around them, barking like a pack of rabid dogs. The girl is shaking from her sloped shoulders to her pale, thick thighs. Her hands cover her face, and a mop of red, frizzy curls obscures what her hands don't. One slice of skin shows at the top of her forehead, bright red beneath a layer of freckles.

For a minute, I don't move. I have this weird, out of body feeling, like I had when we first arrived in Arkansas, and I realized this was real. Now, I have that same feeling, as if I can see my life splitting. There's the girl I was, and the girl I'm about to become. This is my chance to join them. I can hang on the arm of a Darling boy and laugh. Be best friends with the old families. I have the right cars, the right bags and shoes, the right house. I even have the right brothers. I can be one of them. A Darling Doll.

I know how it works. I can fight for a place in this new world, a place at the best table, in the best parking spot. It wouldn't be hard. It would take a bit of adjustment, but everyone would move aside and let me take a spot at the top with the other old-money families, just like someone vacated their seat without complaint when I sat there. I can do this. It's the easy route, the one I took for so long I didn't even realize what kind of person I'd become until it was too late.

Now I have a chance to be someone else. To atone for my sins. To say, no more. This is who I am now. This is Crystal Dolce 2.0. This is the girl I am in Arkansas, the girl I am to these people. My brothers like to make an entrance, but I didn't want to do that today. I wanted to keep my head down at this school, to stay out of trouble and keep quiet. To let someone else have the spotlight.

It's only my first day, and I already know that's not going to happen. Because the truth is, I'm not made for invisibility. I'm not the sweet girl, and no matter how hard I tried, I could never be. Disappearing doesn't come naturally to me any more than it does to my brothers. Being invisible isn't how I'm going to make up for the person I was. Fighting my brothers' battles isn't how. This is how. *This* is my moment.

I wanted a chance to make things right. A way to be better. I wasn't sure how I was going to do that, but now I know. I have a choice to make, a choice that's going to ruin everything I've planned since I heard we were moving to Arkansas. If I do this, I'm not going to be the quiet new girl, the sister of royalty. And I'm not going to be the old Crystal. I thought those were my two choices, but I was wrong. There's a third choice. My choice.

I choose to make waves.

six

I step forward from the crowd. A surge of power rises in me. I'd been so nervous to come here, to try again. Now, the nerves are gone. I'm solid as steel.

"Let her go," I say, my voice quiet and calm but undeniable.

For one moment, Devlin doesn't move, doesn't speak. He stares at me, and I catch the surprise, the incredulity, in his gaze. I take it he's not used to people standing up to him.

"Or what?" he asks, recovering quickly from his surprise and fixing a superior smile on me.

"There is no *or*," I say slowly. "Let her go."

A cat-ear headband lies on the floor at our feet. I kick it aside and step even closer. Glancing down, I realize Devlin's not holding her neck but the back of a dog collar she's wearing.

"You have no idea what's going on here," he says, his blue eyes fixing on mine. "Why don't you mind your own business, or better yet, go back to New York where you belong."

I cross my arms and glare back at him, at those blue eyes that are so clear they look like the surface of a frozen lake in January. Devlin's eyes promise secret dangers that are every bit as deadly as those icy depths.

I tear my gaze away from his and gesture to the trembling girl. "Anyone with two eyes can see what's going on here. Now let her go. I won't ask you again."

Devlin's lips twist into an amused smirk. "I'm afraid you're going to have to," he purrs in that silk-draped voice. "Because this isn't over. Unless you're going to kneel for me instead."

His eyes flick over me, and his smile widens the slightest bit.

"Not if it's the last thing I ever do."

"Kneel, Frosh," he says, powering down on the girl's collar.

She clumsily drops to her knees, and everyone starts laughing and whistling and barking again. For one horrible second, I think he's going to make her blow him right here in the hall.

He called my bluff. I can't make him stop. I don't know this guy. I have nothing on him, and no power in this school. So I do the only thing I can think of—distract him so she can escape. I step in and shove him as hard as I can.

He feels like a brick wall under my palms, but I catch him off guard just enough that he stumbles sideways. His hand is still caught in the girl's dog collar, and she falls sideways onto the floor before his fingers come free. I step over her, getting right in his face. With my back to her, my body is between them, and I hope she has the sense to get the hell out of here. I just played the only card I've got—desperation's best friend, the element of surprise.

It only buys her a few seconds.

Devlin's hand flashes out and grabs me by the throat, and he shoves me up against the lockers before I can jerk away. My body bangs against the metal, the sound echoing down the hall. His eyes flash with fury and his fingers clench around my neck for a split second before he relaxes his grip to one that is less painful but just as effective at restraining me. All the adrenaline that fueled my courage is turning to something else, and I'm shaking so hard he can probably feel it.

"Where do you get off treating people that way?" I ask, spitting the words at him as I claw to free myself from his chokehold. "You think just because you drive a fancy car and wear a big name that you're better than everyone else?"

A cruel smile teases the corners of his lips, and he steps in, his body a whisper away from mine, the heat of it swirling over me like a blinding fog. "I don't think that," he says in that silky voice, his hand still around my throat just tight enough to feel like a threat. He tips my chin up, his warm breath caressing my lips when he speaks. "I know it."

For a second, I can't move, as if the ice of his crystal blue gaze has frozen me solid even as a fire rages under my skin. My body is a contradiction, confusion slashing through me. I can't tell if I feel incredibly, addictively strong, or terrifyingly weak. If the thing awakening in the core of my being is a delicate bud, a tender green sprout that can be trampled by one careless boot, or a fire-breathing dragon that could raze the earth with her fury.

"This one," he says slowly, his voice raised but his eyes still locked on mine. "Is now the Darling Dog."

A hush falls over the crowd, and then a burst of whispers. Before I can spit in his eye for calling me a dog, a fist connects with the side of his head, sending him reeling sideways and tearing me from his grip. King grabs Devlin by the throat before he can recover. "What the fuck are you doing to my sister?"

What the fuck, indeed.

As fists fly, I flatten my back against the lockers, pressing my burning palms against the cool metal, my heart stampeding in my chest. I close my eyes and breathe. I'm not shocked by the appearance of one of my brothers. In the recesses of my mind, I was probably even expecting it. Waiting for them to show up for me, the way they always do.

When I open my eyes, King and Devlin are both on their feet. King is bigger and stronger, but Devlin is quicker on his feet, dancing like a boxer as he throws a punch. It slams into King's jaw, and he stumbles backward. Royal bursts from the crowd and tackles Devlin. They slam into King, and the three of them go down together. The third Darling boy, the one I haven't met, dives into the fray.

I edge away from the fight, only to run into Colt Darling. He gives me a crooked grin and drawls, "Now look what you've gone and done, Crystal Sweet."

"Me?"

"Naughty girl," he says. "I like it."

"Shouldn't you be helping your cousins?" I ask. "Because no offense to your fam, but I'm pretty sure my brothers are kicking their asses right now."

"I'm a lover, not a fighter," he says, flicking his shiny hair off his forehead.

I spot a mop of red hair in the crowd, a pair of black ears poking up from the curls. I can't believe that girl's not locked in a bathroom stall sobbing right now. "I have to go," I say, edging away from Colt.

"Don't run away yet," he says. "We're still brawling."

"*We're* not doing anything," I say. "And I need to find my friend."

"I'm your friend," Colt says, placing a hand over his heart and giving me puppy dog eyes.

"Not after this," I say, watching as the twins shove their way through and join the fight. I feel a little bad for the Darlings, and I'm definitely not sticking around to watch the beating.

I try to step around Colt, but he steps in front of me again. "Who's your friend?" he asks, crossing his arms over his chest and narrowing his eyes.

"Her," I say in annoyance, pointing to the redhead.

"Dixie?

"Yeah." I elbow my way toward the redhead, leaving Colt behind.

"What the hell are you doing here?" I ask, grabbing Dixie's elbow.

She turns to me, her eyes wide as saucers. "What?"

"I created a distraction, and you're just going to stand here and watch?"

"That's what you were doing?"

"It worked, didn't it?" I ask, pulling her away from the crowd and down the hall as a couple teachers come running.

"You started a brawl?" Dixie asks, still gaping. "On purpose?"

The answer that comes automatically to my lips is a cool smirk and a shrug of indifference.

But then I remember that I'm trying to shed my bitch skin, so I admit the truth instead. "Not exactly. I was just trying to get them to leave you alone."

Dixie stops short. "Why would you do that?"

I search for an excuse, but nothing comes. "Let's just say I haven't always been a very nice person. Maybe I wanted to make up for it in some way."

"And you're going to do that by being my friend?" she asks, looking a bit too… *Everything.* Hopeful, and scared, and horribly, desperately transparent. This poor girl obviously has no idea how the game is played. Because that's all life is—a game. Some people are dealt better hands, sure, but we're all players on the same giant chessboard. Or football field, or whatever plane you want to use. Even the players dealt the best cards can lose it all with one ill-planned move, and the next thing you know, you've got nothing.

I don't know what hand this girl was dealt, or what cards she's holding now, but I know she needs help figuring it out. And I'm going to be the one who helps her.

"Tell you what," I say. "I'm new here, but you're not. I could use some help learning the ropes. So how about we make a deal?"

Dixie's eyes widen. "You're bribing me to be your friend?"

"How long have you gone to school here?"

"T-This is my first year," she stutters.

I remember Devlin calling her Frosh, and I realize she's only a freshman. "How long have you lived in this town?"

"All my life," she says. She has a soft, breathy voice with a sweet accent like the Darlings. "I'm actually the mayor's step-niece, which is why I go here. Not that he'd acknowledge me. I mean, at holidays and stuff my parents make me go schmooze, but otherwise, they pretend they don't know me. Last time we visited, his wife told my parents not to bring me over looking so 'unkempt.' But really I think it's because I'm fat."

"Well, I could use a friend," I say, deciding to process her words slowly when I have a chance. "And judging by what I just witnessed, you could, too. Why didn't anyone stand up for you?"

"I'm new here," she says. "I mean, all the freshmen are new, obviously. But they all went to private school together and then came here for high school. I went to public school until this year. I haven't really... I mean, I don't really have any friends."

She's about as red as when the Darling had her on her knees. I feel bad for asking about her friends, since I obviously embarrassed her.

"You have a friend now," I say. "Meet me in the dining hall for lunch." With the way things are going today, though, I'm not sure any of the Dolces will make it until lunch.

seven

I did it. Something better. Or at least I tried. But what happens when your good deed leads to people being hurt? As they say, the road to hell is paved with those good intentions. I know plenty about the road to hell—with cruel intentions. Let's hope this good deed doesn't land me in a hell of my own making. Because right now? It feels less like a good deed and more like social suicide.

I make it halfway through the next period before the headmaster calls me down so I can tell him my version of the fight. I wasn't involved, so they can't do shit to me. I feign ignorance, saying it was all a misunderstanding. When they let me go, I search the office for signs of my brothers or the Darlings, but no one offers me a clue.

At lunch, I hurry across the open space of the commons, scanning for my brothers. But I see only strangers throwing a frisbee on the lawn, a few jumping bikes up and down a wide set of steps, and more milling around talking to their friends or sitting on the edge of the fountain. I reach the dining hall, a modern, angular building that's all steel and glass from the outside. Inside, it's all exposed beams and bamboo and no Dolce boys.

Surely they aren't still talking to the headmaster. Unless…

My heart lurches in my chest. I'm always telling Royal to take it easy, that one day he's going to get into it with the wrong person, the one who will file charges. Or that he'll seriously hurt himself or someone else. Maybe even, by accident, do more than hurt them.

I gulp down my growing panic, take out my phone, and send a quick text.

When I look up, I catch sight of the third Darling boy, the one I haven't talked to. I storm over to his table. A few kids snicker and woof at me, but I ignore them. The Darling is talking and laughing like nothing had happened, though a dark bruise is forming on his chiseled cheekbone and one eye is swollen half closed.

I slap my palm down on the round table. The group sitting there falls silent, glancing at me before turning expectantly to the Darling.

"Where are my brothers?" I ask.

The table is full, about ten people sitting with him, a mixture of athletic looking guys and pretty girls. *Darling Dolls*, I remember Lacey calling them. But I don't let my curiosity distract me. I keep my eyes fixed on the Darling boy.

He grins and pushes back from the table, lounging in his seat with one arm dangling over the back of his chair. It's a pose that makes it nearly impossible not to stare at his crotch.

"Hey, it's the new bitch," he says. "Sweetie, is it? That's a good name for a dog."

His friends snicker, but I keep my eyes on the one who spoke. I don't want to be feared or envied or hated at Willow Heights. I just want to be quietly respected. That's enough for me.

Apparently, these guys have other plans.

If they won't let me have it my way, I'll have to play their game. And I intend to win. "It's Dolce," I say, my voice as brittle as my first name. "You're going to want to remember that."

"I'm Preston," he says without missing a beat. "You'll want to remember that, too, so you can scream it while you cum."

I'm the one who misses a beat. I may have run shit in Manhattan, but I had a team to back me up. Here, I'm not calling the plays anymore. And Preston knows it. The glint of malicious triumph in his eyes says as much.

He leans forward the slightest bit, his eyes hot on mine. "If you're looking for a seat, I've got one for you."

He runs one finger slowly up the front of his pants, and my eyes follow it with a kind of trancelike fascination. My heart is trembling in my chest by the time his finger stops. I gulp, staring at the slight bulge I can make out under the navy slacks.

He leans forward another inch, lowers his voice to a conspiratorial murmur, and says, "On my tip."

I can feel heat prickling up my neck as I struggle for a comeback. Sure, there are assholes in Manhattan. But at our school? A guy would gouge out his own eyeballs before he'd speak to me that way. He'd know that I was off limits, that my brothers would murder him for messing with me.

Suddenly, I realize how wrong my brothers were. Even Daddy. Willow Heights isn't some sad little shit hole. Faulkner isn't a pathetic hick town. It's a place where my name holds no power, where my family is no better than anyone else's. It's a place where I have no protection. Where I'm vulnerable.

Whatever I say to Preston won't help. It will probably make it worse. I'll be the hysterical psycho who lost it in the café, the chick who can't take a joke. I refuse to sink to his level. Dolces have more class in one fingernail than this asshole has in his entire family. So I simply straighten, turn, and walk away with my head held high and whatever dignity I have left. Behind me, I hear hoots of laughter and people slapping Preston's back, smacking the table at the hilarity.

"Come on, baby," Preston calls after me. "I hear city girls have all the moves. Bounce on it like a pro."

I realize the cafeteria has fallen silent, that everyone is watching the exchange. Waiting.

It's not until I'm halfway to the door that I realize what they're waiting for. From the corner of my eye, I see kids elbowing each other, relaying a message Preston must have sent with some signal behind my back. As I pass each table, everyone sitting there barks at me. It's not a silly little sound, either. It's that feral, dangerous noise deep in their throats, like Rottweilers on the defensive.

My knees are shaking by the time I reach the door. All I want to do is run to the nearest bathroom, lock myself inside, and let out the flood of tears threatening behind my eyes.

But then I remember that I told Dixie I'd meet her for lunch. I stop and take a deep breath, balling my hands into fists. I can run away and tell my brothers that someone was mean to me, like a baby, or I can be a big girl and stand my ground. I'm not going back over there to make a scene, tell him what a piece of shit he is. But I'm also not going to run away. Because if I run now, I'll never stop running from them. They'll drag me deeper and deeper into hell, laughing all the way, and they won't stop until I make them.

So I'm stopping them right now.

I turn at the door. I draw myself up, and I swallow my pride, and I let my eyes sweep the dining hall until I find Dixie sitting at a table in the corner. She waves to me. A big grin stretches across her face when I see her, and she frantically gestures me over. Forcing my eyes not to return to the Darling table, not to beg him to call off the school, I walk toward her. I keep my gait even, not hurrying but not strolling too slowly and giving them an extra second to bark at me.

They're all watching me, waiting to see what I'll do. I won't give them the satisfaction of a show. I slide in next to Dixie and let out a slow breath.

"Tough school," I say, keeping my words careful, too. I don't know this girl. Yes, she wears her heart on her sleeve, but for all I know, she's a Darling.

She grabs my arm and lowers her voice, her eyes shining with excitement. "Did you just talk to Preston Darling?"

"Yes," I say, detaching my arm from her grip. "What about it?"

"He's *Preston Darling*," she squeals like she's talking about Ed Sheeran or Brody Villines instead of a high school boy in Nowhere, Arkansas.

"Okay," I say slowly. "You really need to stop saying it like that. Have you forgotten what his cousin did to you this morning?"

"No," she says, touching her headband. Looking at it again, I see that it's a pair of dog ears. Along with the dog collar, it makes her an easy target. "What did he say to you?"

"Nothing." I cut my eyes at the silly headband. "Why do you wear that?"

"I have to," she says, an edge of defiance in her voice.

"Why?"

"Because they told me to," she says, her eyes widening.

"Wait a second," I say, holding up a hand. That sounds a little too familiar, and a sick feeling rises in my stomach. Just when I think I've figured it out, something comes along to turn my perception of this place on its head. "The Darlings tell you what to wear? Why? Are you related to them?"

"Oh, gosh, no." She chews at a hangnail, shrinking in her seat and eyeing me nervously.

"Why?" I ask again, my eyes narrowing.

"I have to be obedient," she says. "I'm this year's Darling Dog. Or… I was. I guess now you are. There's only one at a time." She cowers as if she expects me to be pissed that I inadvertently made waves and therefore took her spot as the Darlings' victim.

I remember Devlin telling the crowd that I was a Darling Dog, and my stomach roils. If they think they're going to tell me what to wear, they've got another thing coming. But I can't stop the rest of it. The barking. The crude taunts.

The bullying.

The irony is not lost on me. When I said I was going to atone for my sins, I didn't think I'd have to go this far. I thought I could start over, be someone better. I thought I could stick up for someone instead of participating in their downfall. But suddenly, I know this is the only way to truly pay for my sins. I have to see what it's like on the other side. To see how it feels to tumble from the throne, to look up at it from below.

But I won't make it easy for them. I may be forced to kneel, but I won't do it on my own. I won't wear their collars and bow at their feet. I'll fight every step of the way. Because no matter how far they bend me to their will, I will never break.

eight

Turns out, it wasn't as simple as moving to a new school and taking over like royalty. Turns out, even small towns have kings. And those kings don't want to cede their thrones.

"What happened?" I ask, sliding into the front seat of the Range Rover that afternoon. "Where were you at lunch?"

"That asshole tried to suspend us," King says, shifting into gear. "Buckle up."

I obey before turning to my brother. "Wait, did you actually get in trouble?"

My brothers don't get in trouble. Of course, they usually don't throw down in the middle of the hall, but it was a good show of dominance on their first day. Still, we never get in trouble. School officials turn a blind eye to people like us.

Or they did in Manhattan.

"We took off the rest of the day," King says. "Dad went down to take care of it. We'll be back tomorrow."

"Oh," I say with a sigh of relief. At least I had Dixie to sit with at lunch. Yes, she's a total Darling fangirl, but at least I had someone. Even if she's someone who went super nerd on me and got out an actual notebook and made me brainstorm "The Rules of Friendship" with her, she's nice. I chose her for a friend, and I'm sticking to it, rules and all.

"How was it?" King asks, swinging out of the lot.

I open my mouth to tell him, but then I shut it. I don't want to start another fight, to get my brothers in trouble before the school has time to realize we're just as untouchable as the Darlings. And I don't want to be in the middle of the what my brothers have going on with them. That's something different from what happened to me today. The dust will settle soon enough, and if I don't give the Darlings the satisfaction of reacting, maybe they'll get bored and move on. Some other new girl will come along, and I'll be old news.

A funny little twist tugs inside me at the thought. I push it away. I swore I'd be good this time. I've had the limelight. I don't need it again.

"Maybe Daddy hasn't made a big enough donation," I say to King.

King smirks. "He did today."

"Good," I say, but a flutter of uncertainty tickles my ribs from within. Maybe pushing back against the Darlings isn't such a good idea. Maybe we should join them instead of fighting them. I know better than to suggest that to King. My brothers have set their sights on ruling this town, and there's no stopping them now. If the Darlings had reacted differently, if they'd been even a little bit welcoming, my brothers might have opened ranks enough to allow them in. They might have considered the Darlings worthy. But it's too late now.

King pats my knee as we pull up to our house. "Hope you're ready," he says. "Tomorrow we're going in swinging."

*

The next day, my brothers are allowed back at school. I've given up on being someone I'm not, and the fear I felt the day before is gone. I'm not a shrinking violet, and I couldn't be if I tried. Now that I have the attention of Willow Heights, I just have to turn it to something positive, use it to do good and help people.

We leave the house early, which is unlike us. An undercurrent of tension in the car makes me jittery, but my brothers assure me everything is fine. When we pull up to Willow Heights, King swings the Rover into the first parking spot, the one near the walkway.

"What are you doing?" I ask slowly.

"We're taking what's ours," King says, shutting off the engine.

"And you couldn't have told me?" I ask, climbing out. "Devlin's going to lose it."

"Here's hoping," Duke says, draping an arm over my shoulder. "I can't wait to see the look on that asshole's face when he realizes we outbid him for this."

"Next, we take their spots on the football team," King says.

I roll my eyes. "You're not going to quit, are you?"

"Fuck no," Baron says, holding up a hand for Duke to slap.

"We're making a point," King says. "When they back off and realize we're here to stay, that we own this school now, we'll have no problem with them. But first they have to accept that there's a new rule in this town."

"And if they ever touch you again, I'll fucking kill them," Royal growls behind me.

I turn to him, and like always, it steadies my mind. This crazy plan, this crazy prank, doesn't seem too crazy if he's on board with it. His dark gaze holds mine, and I center myself. Royal squeezes my hand for a second before his eyes focus on something behind me. I hear the roar of an engine, and before I even look, I know the Darlings have arrived.

The Bel Air skids to a stop so suddenly that a shriek of brakes sounds, and white smoke drifts up from the tires.

Devlin is out of the car and in our faces in two seconds flat, the door hanging open and the engine still running.

"What the fuck is this?" he demands, looking at the Rover like it's some old beater car. I know it's not the car he objects to, though. It's us. Our new money. Our power. Our claim to a throne he once ascended. A throne he thought he'd always own because of his name.

"This is our parking spot," King says calmly.

Devlin isn't calm. He grabs King, and I scoot away, ready for another brawl. These Arkansas kids have short fuses. Royal likes to fight more than can possibly be healthy, but he doesn't lose his temper. We know how to take shit without letting it ruffle us. The Darlings? They don't even try.

They throw punches first, ask questions never.

Devlin's fist connects with King's jaw before he leaps back, dancing on his toes like a boxer. "There's more where that came from," Devlin snarls. "Get back in your car and go park where you were yesterday, over there with the trash. That's where your family belongs."

King spits blood at Devlin's feet. "Take it up with your admin. They know we belong right here. And pretty soon you'll know it, too."

A dozen or so kids have gathered to watch the standoff. Preston hops from the Bel Air to back his brother, and even Colt climbs out. The toes of his cowboy boots peek out from the hem of his slacks, and I can't help but wonder if he was thinking of me this morning. The thought makes a little charge go through me. I thought they'd look cheesy, but somehow, he makes it look good. He grins when he catches me checking him out, and I pull my attention away from him.

A huge, cotton candy-pink truck hops the curb and comes roaring into the parking lot and pulls into the space next to ours. I gape at the bubblegum monstrosity, but no one else seems surprised by the vehicle or the cartoon who stumbles out of it. She barely keeps her feet, grabbing onto her truck bed to steady herself on her six-inch heels. Her leather, hot-pink skirt barely covers her ass, and her enormous breasts strain against a white button-up shirt.

"Sorry, y'all," she says in a breathy, sweet southern accent. "Did I interrupt somethin'?" She shakes soft, platinum curls back from her face and looks around at us.

"No," Devlin snaps before turning and storming into the building.

Redneck Barbie gives us a wounded look, then strides past us, calling after Devlin. Preston steps into the Bel Air and pulls off to park somewhere else, and the crowd begins to disperse. Somehow, I don't think this is over, though.

"That's Dolly," a conspiratorial murmur tickles my ear. I look up to see Colt behind me. He nods at the retreating figure of the Barbie girl and shoots me that lazy grin. "She's got a thing for Devlin, if you couldn't tell."

I lean away from Colt, but judging by the look on King's face, he saw Colt's fingers brush the curve of my waist. I scowl at the friendly Darling cousin. It wouldn't be fair to let this guy think we're friends. Cutting him off quickly and thoroughly is the only way to go.

"I thought I was a dog," I say. "You'd better go set up in the hall so you can bark at me when I walk in."

"Aw, don't be sore at me," he says. "I didn't call you that. Besides, everybody likes dogs. They're cute as hell."

"Why are you talking to our sister?" Duke asks, sliding in at to my side and standing over me the way my brothers always do.

One look at them was enough to make most guys back home back off, but Colt just grins. "Last I checked, it's a free country," he says. "I figure I got as much right to talk to a pretty girl as the next guy."

"You figured wrong," Royal says, stepping up to my other side, jostling Colt out of the way in the process. "Now back the fuck off. Crystal is not available."

"Understood," Colt says, raising both hands and stepping back. "See you in second period, Sugar Crystal."

He gives me a wink before turning and sauntering off.

"Who the fuck is that?" Royal asks, getting up in my face. If he wasn't my brother, I'd be scared of him. With his thick dark brows drawn together, he looks dangerous as a hurricane.

I shrug, my heart hammering as the words fall from my lips. "No one. We got paired up in class. That's it." I won't say I've never lied to my brothers, but it's not a frequent occurrence. But for some reason, I can't bring myself to tell the whole truth. Because the truth is, I don't know if that's it or not. The truth is, I feel some pull to the magnetism of the Darlings. They are like us, but not like us. I want to know how other people like us run their school, what's different and what's not. I want to know why Colt is so casually fearless and why Devlin is so angry.

"Well, tell your teacher you can't work with him," King says flatly. "We're not getting friendly with that family. We're taking them down."

It's not really a choice. It's not like I'll pick Colt Darling over my own family. My family is everything to me. They might smother me at times or control me more than I'd like, but they're family. They'd die for me.

I've known Colt for one day.

"Okay," I say, nodding. Losing Colt's friendship is not a high price to pay for being a Dolce. Loyalty is everything to us, and we need to show that. Letting people see me talking to a Darling boy is not going to do us any favors. We have to form a united front, to appear as one unit. After all, the Dolce family has a reputation to build.

Still, a small ache forms in my chest when I walk away without an explanation to Colt, without so much as a backwards glance. He's just flirting. He doesn't care about me. And I barely know him, so I can't care about him. But the thought of losing any friend in this hostile place is unsettling. Not to mention that maybe, for once in my life, it would be nice to think of myself first. To not have to worry about what it will look like, whether my brothers approve, or how it will reflect on our family.

I push the thoughts away and head to class. This time, I walk with my brothers. No one barks at me, and I hope against my better judgment that it's a first-day initiation, that it'll be forgotten altogether when everyone hears about the fight that almost went down in the parking lot.

And then I walk into first period and see Devlin Darling sitting at the lab table in the back of the room where Mr. Wagnall assigned me the day before.

Fuck no. Not happening.

I turn to the teacher, an older man with little round spectacles and a bald head with tufts of hair that stick out above his ears, making him look exactly like an owl. "Can I sit somewhere else today?"

"Have a seat in your assigned spot," he drones, sounding bored.

"Yeah, see, that guy wasn't here yesterday," I say. "And I'm not supposed to sit with him. Family feud thing. Can I just sit over there?" I gesture to an empty table and give Mr. Wagnall my most charming smile.

"Nice try, Miss Dolce," he says. "But we have assigned seats. Please take yours."

"You'll be hearing from my father."

"I have no doubt," he says, not sounding at all impressed.

The room is filling, and I don't want to make a spectacle, so I grit my teeth and make my way toward Devlin. I hold my head high and keep my eyes forward, my face still. I practice a technique I learned in therapy, picturing myself from the outside. No one can tell my heart is racing and my stomach is knotted with dread, waiting for the barking and name-calling. To everyone else, I'm a pretty girl with flawlessly straightened hair, plum lipstick, and a fitted, conservative dress with a belt and matching pumps.

Everyone is watching me. Silent. Waiting. I pray they can't see my knees shaking and thank heaven they don't make a move. I arrive at Devlin's table, a raised, black-surfaced lab station. Devlin stares at me. "Are you fucking kidding me?" he mutters under his breath. "This is the seat you chose?"

"You weren't here yesterday," I say, sliding onto the stool beside him. "I didn't know you sat here. And Mr. Wagnall says we have assigned seats."

Devlin smirks. "And you just do what everyone tells you, like a good dog?"

I cross my arms over my chest and glare. "I tried. He refused. Do you really think I want to sit with *you?*"

A flicker of surprise flashes in his devastating blue eyes. Apparently, he's not used to girls not falling for his asshole act.

"Then go sit somewhere else," he grinds out.

I shrug. "Not worth a detention. But I hear your family has a lot of sway in this town. Why don't you show me how it's done?"

Devlin's eyes narrow. Then he pushes back from the high table. "Mr. Wagnall? I need a new partner."

Mr. Wagnall sighs and runs a hand over his bald head, closing his eyes for a second like he's praying for patience.

"Fine," he says. "Dolly's partner is out today. You can work with her."

Devlin stills, his hand clenched around the edge of the table. He stares at Mr. Wagnall for a long moment, then shakes his head almost imperceptibly. "Never mind."

Mr. Wagnall sighs and starts droning on about our chemistry assignment.

"Wow," I say. "What'd Redneck Barbie do to piss you off?"

"Don't call her that," Devlin snaps.

I'm too surprised by his defending her to answer. Dolly is slumped in her chair, her head down, her big blonde waves falling forward to hide her face. Suddenly, I feel like shit for saying anything about her. Colt already told me she liked Devlin, though the feeling is definitely not mutual. There's obviously a history there that I know nothing about, so I drop the subject.

"Hey, at least he was going to move you," I offer.

Devlin's smirk returns, and for some reason, a surge of elation rises in me. I did that. I turned his anger off. "You act surprised," he says, his eyes hooded as he watches me.

"Not surprised," I say. "Just confirmed what I already suspected."

"And what's that?"

"That the South works a lot like the mafia."

This time, Devlin's lips twitch like he's holding back a laugh. "I gotta hear this."

I shrug and pull out the supplies we're supposed to be working with. "The Families have all the sway," I say. "They can do whatever they want. It's more about old family loyalties than bottomless pockets."

He's watching me now, his eyes guarded but curiosity showing through.

I toss my dark hair back and give him a serene smile. "Tell me I'm wrong."

"Your family's in the mafia?" he asks.

For some reason, that question reassures me. I get that question a lot. It's nice to know that under it all, Devlin is human just like all of us. Just like me.

I shrug. "We have sway."

He smiles a little, shakes his head, and pulls the experiment instructions in front of him. For the rest of class, I'm dying to ask him questions about his family, to find out what he thinks of what I said, what he thinks about us living next door, why he was out throwing a football at midnight. But I remind myself that I'm not supposed to care about the answers to any of those questions. The only reason I should be talking to Devlin Darling at all is to find out information that can take him down.

That's still being better than I used to be, right? I mean, taking someone down... That sounds like something Veronica would do. Something I did before. But this is different.

This isn't hurting someone small who can't or won't fight back. This is taking down the kind of person who picks on people like that. Taking down a bully is nothing to feel guilty about, especially when I know my brothers will take their place. And my brothers aren't angels, but they're not bullies. The twins might be manwhores, and Royal itches for a fight the way addicts itch for a fix. But they don't collar a girl and call her the school dog. They don't get their power by making someone else feel small and helpless.

What we're doing is taking over and making the school better. That's a noble goal. Next year, there will be no dog packs in the halls of Willow Heights. It will be safe for people like Dixie. Safe from people like the Darlings and the person I used to be.

nine

Coming into a new school and starting at the top means pushing everyone below you down a step. It means climbing over every single person to get there. The person at the top has highest to fall. Maybe nothing changes at all for the person at the bottom. They're still there. Only maybe it does. Maybe you take a hand reaching up from the very bottom of the pile and you pull them up with you.

Tell me it doesn't change things for them. Tell me. I dare you.

The rest of the morning passes uneventfully. Preston is in my math class, which is a mix of sophomores and juniors, but he doesn't seem to notice me today. A couple people give me dirty looks, but no one barks at me. Halfway through class, Preston gets up and walks out without a word to the teacher.

A few minutes later, Dolly raises her hand and asks to use the restroom. Neither of them returns to class.

I wonder if they're hooking up. And if Devlin knows. And why I care.

I turn my attention back to the lesson and make it to lunch without issue. There, I head straight for Dixie's table. She's wearing the dog collar and ears from the day before, along with a black top that shows ample, freckled cleavage. I slide into a seat next to her.

"So," I start. "Tell me more about this Darling Dogs and Darling Dolls thing."

She looks taken aback by my question. I can't tell if she's surprised that I asked, or that I sat with her again, or some other reason.

Before she can answer, the Dolce boys arrive, towering over our table.

"What are you doing?" King asks.

"Sitting with my friend," I say flatly. For some fucked up reason, I feel bonded to her because of the stupid Darling Dog label.

King jerks his chin toward the next table, which sits empty. "Can we talk?"

I sigh and stand, following them to the empty table. "I gave up the whole being a wallflower plan," I say. "I admit, it was stupid. But I'm not going to be a bitch, either. I like Dixie. And she needs me."

"You're punishing yourself for what happened in New York by making over that girl?" Royal asks, hitting way too close to home.

"No," I say with a scowl.

"She's a dog," Duke says.

"A what?" I ask, my heart lurching. Do they know about that? And that I've taken over that title from her?

"Ugly," Baron says. "She doesn't take care of herself. If she put in a little effort, she'd be okay. Nice tits."

"You're gross," I say. "And against the rules."

Since they basically reject any guy I'd even consider while they can fuck anyone they want, I made them swear my friends were the exception. No dating them, no hooking up, no talking about their tits.

"Fine," Duke says. "But do you really want to start off like this? I don't see her as a social climber. We're going places, and she's going to hold you back."

I cross my arms and stare at him, refusing to back down. "Either she comes with me, or I'm not going anywhere."

"Fine," King says. "Have it your way. But you're making more work for yourself."

"I'm not afraid of hard work," I say. "Besides, she knows this school. She's lived in this town all her life. Maybe she can help us. And I know I can help her."

"Then let's sit with her," Royal says with a shrug. My brothers all take seats around the table with Dixie, who looks like she's about to have a heart attack. Her face turns red, and she stutters through my introductions. She barely says a word for the entire lunch while my brothers discuss trying out for the football team. The season's already started, but Dad's influence can get them at least a tryout.

"Who starts?" King asks Dixie.

"What?" she asks, her eyes going wide. "Oh, I... The Darlings, obviously. And... them." She gestures vaguely to a table where I spot the three cousins and their crowd.

"Once we're on the team, we'll prove ourselves," Royal says, glaring at the Darlings. "We'll see who's starting then."

"They're really good," Dixie says.

"You haven't seen us play," Duke says with a smirk.

"You should come to the game on Friday," Dixie says. A blush sweeps over her cheeks, and she shoves a bite of sandwich into her mouth.

"Sounds good," Duke says. "We can scope out the competition."

"By next week, there won't be competition," King says.

When lunch ends, Devlin and Preston swagger by, beautiful blondes swarming around them like flies. Devlin catches sight of us and snickers. "Is that the best you can do?" he asks.

"You can't even get our leftovers," Preston says, laughing at my brothers. "The only girls who want you are the dogs and your own sister."

They walk out laughing. Even Colt grins as he strolls after them. I glance sideways at Dixie, who's gone red as a lobster again.

"He'll be eating his words soon enough," Duke says with a grin. "When we're fucking all their girlfriends."

My brothers go off to class, and Dixie grabs my arm. "Oh. My. God. Those are your *brothers*?"

"Yes," I say, rolling my eyes. "And no, I can't set you up with them." This is one thing that hasn't changed. I'm used to this line of questioning. I'm used to girls trying to get close to me just to get to my brothers. I'm used to them dumping me when they find out my brothers won't date my friends.

"Oh, I wasn't…" Dixie gets all red and flustered again. "I mean, they wouldn't go out with me."

"Why not?" I ask.

"Because," she says, widening her eyes at me like it's obvious, like I should know why.

I shrug. "They don't date my friends. So if that's what you're after, let's skip the pretense of friendship, and you can go after them. Going through me to get to them isn't going to work."

"I'm not." Dixie draws back, and I realize I slipped into defensive mode without meaning to, that I'm being a total bitch.

"I'm sorry," I say with a sigh. "It just happened one too many times. When a girl starts being nice to me for no reason, I assume. Which is shitty, and I should work on that."

"You're suspicious when people are nice to you?"

I can't help but laugh. "Fucked up, right? But also pretty typical for my old school."

"Wow," she says, shaking her head. "Does that mean… I mean, you're being nice to me. Should I be suspicious? Because you probably shouldn't be friends with me. I'm the Darling Dog, and you… You could be, like, a Doll and the head cheerleader all at once."

"Been there, done that," I say. "I'm ready for a change."

"But you're gorgeous," she says, her face flushing. "I'm not even pretty."

"Shut up," I say. "You're pretty."

She ducks her head, shaking it back and forth. "Look at me. I've never even had a boyfriend. The only reason I go here is because my aunt married the mayor."

"First off, I've never had a boyfriend, either. And secondly, who says you're not pretty? The Darlings? Fuck them. My brother thinks you're sexy."

"What?" she squeaks, skidding to a stop in the hall. "He said that?"

I shrug. "Okay, he said something rude about your tits, but that's what he meant."

"Really?" Dixie's practically glowing as she adjusts her boobs, pushing them up and adjusting her bra.

"This school is fucked up," I say. "Don't put too much stock in what people here think. This whole town is backwards."

She seems to think about this for a minute before nodding and continuing down the hall. I fall into step beside her.

"So, I'm the Darling Dog now? What exactly does that entail?"

"Well, different things," Dixie says, blushing again. "Actually, I should probably give these back now that you've been claimed…" She trails off and touches her dog ears.

"Don't tell me you're sorry that you've passed on the title to me."

"No," she says quickly. "I'm not. Here." She yanks off the headband and reaches back to unsnap her dog collar.

"They'd probably be mad if they saw me wearing them now that they took away my title, anyway. It's better if I give them to you."

"You can put them right there," I say, pointing to a trash can.

Dixie's eyes widen. "Devlin Darling put this collar on me. I can't just throw it away."

"Then let me," I say, plucking the items from her hand and depositing them exactly where they belong. I brush off my hands and turn back to her. "Now that we've taken care of that, tell me more about the football team."

That afternoon, I fill in the details for my brothers, telling them everything I learned from Dixie. A tiny pang of guilt accompanies my divulgence, as if I owe the Darlings something. Which I don't. Two of them have been complete assholes to me, and Colt… Well, I don't know about Colt. But I certainly don't owe him loyalty. These are my brothers, and I want them to have everything they want. And they want everything.

As I talk, we turn into our neighborhood and curve along the narrow, one-lane asphalt road toward our new home. I push the guilt away. I'm not telling my brothers anything they couldn't find out by asking around the way that I have. And I like helping them.

We're just passing the Darling's driveway when the Range Rover jerks wildly. King yanks the wheel straight, and the twins shout a chorus of curses as another jolt goes through it. The car skids sideways, the wheel sinking into the shoulder before the car slams to a halt against the brick monstrosities that serve as mailboxes around here. Ours and the Darlings are side by side, right between the two properties, and we managed to topple both. Judging by the solidity of the mailboxes, we probably just totaled the Range Rover, too.

"What the fuck," King fumes, leaping out of the car.

I can hear the air whistling out of the punctured tire, but I'm too stunned to move for a second. The twins keep up a solid stream of cursing as they jump out of the car to look at the tire, too.

"You okay?" Royal asks, adjusting the mirror to see me.

"Fine," I say, taking a deep breath and running my damp palms over my thighs. "It's just a flat."

"There's fucking nails in the road," Duke yells.

King ducks back into the car, gripping the steering wheel and staring straight ahead, his jaw clenched and his knuckles white.

"What happened?" I ask, wrapping my hands around my knees and squeezing until my nails bite into my skin. "Can you change the tire?"

"Go up to the house," King says, not moving a muscle.

"We don't have three spares," Baron says, dropping into the seat beside me.

A door slams, and I turn to see a thin, blonde woman emerging from the Darling's house. She's wearing hot pink capri pants and a flowered blouse, her hair pulled up in a high, smooth pony. She starts toward us with mincing steps on her pink high heels, making her way carefully down the white gravel walkway between the bowing trees. Her hips sway as she takes each tiny step, a phone in one hand and what looks like a pie balanced on the other.

"Tootle-oo," she calls, waving at us with the hand holding the phone.

Royal curses under his breath, hauling himself out of the passenger side. The rest of us climb out as well, since it's obvious the Range Rover isn't going anywhere right now. Duke whistles softly, his eyes locked on the twitching hips of the woman approaching. "If that's Devlin's mom, it won't even be taking one for the team to fuck her."

"Do you think it was them?" I ask. As if in answer, a powder blue Bel Air turns into the neighborhood and rolls up behind us. The top is down, his blond hair tousled, his arm resting along the windowsill of the car. A pair of designer shades cover his mean eyes. He looks like something straight out of a movie, especially when he flashes us a smug grin. "Car trouble?" he drawls, not moving to get out of his convertible.

"Oh, there you are, darling," calls the woman as she reaches the end of their drive and starts for our car. "I've been meaning to go meet the neighbors all week. Let's introduce ourselves."

Devlin doesn't answer. He sits in the car for a minute, and I think he's going to tell her no. Just as it begins to get awkward, though, he swings open the door and steps out. His mother tilts her head, and he leans in and gives her a quick kiss on the cheek. I'm touched, not to mention surprised as hell. The way this guy acts at school, I'd never have pegged him as a mama's boy. She doesn't look old enough to be his mother, either, but appearances are deceiving. If I learned anything from Mom's friends, it's the lengths women will go to in order to appear youthful.

"Y'all must be the Dolce clan," she says, apparently satisfied with Devlin's display of affection. She sashays past him and over to us. A pair of sunglasses sit perched on her nose, so I can't fully read her expression as she takes us in.

"That's us," King says, thrusting out a hand. "I'm King Dolce."

"The king of the Dolce clan?" she asks, then titters at her own joke.

I force a smile and intercept before she can get all gross the way older women do about my brothers. "You must be Mrs. Darling," I say, holding out a hand. "I'm Crystal Dolce."

She plunks the glass pie dish into my hands. "It's lovely to meet you, Crystal," she says. "Why don't you run this up to the house and bring your daddy down to take a look at these mailboxes while we introduce ourselves?"

My jaw nearly hits the pavement as I gape at her.

What. The. Actual. Fuck.

Not seeming to realize she's just been rude as hell, or more likely not giving a fuck, Mrs. Darling turns to slide her thin, tan fingers into King's. "Well, hello there. I'm Mrs. Darling, your next-door neighbor." She smiles adoringly at him before reaching past me to shake Royal's hand, so close I have to sidestep so I don't get knocked over. Devlin stands behind her, a bored smirk on his lips. I wish I could see his eyes behind his shades, see what he thinks about his mother being so obvious in her flirtation with my brothers.

Royal shakes her hand before stepping over to join me. "Looks good," he murmurs, glancing at the pie. "Aren't you going to run along so the adults can talk?"

"Shut up," I say, elbowing him and trying not to laugh. I'm so grateful for him always noticing when I need his quiet support and always being there to give it without me even asking.

When Mrs. Darling tries to introduce Devlin, he nods at us. "We met at school," is all he says.

"My goodness, what happened here?" she asks, gesturing to the pile of bricks where the mailboxes stood.

"Just a little accident," King says, sounding so unconcerned that you'd never know five minutes ago he looked like a bomb about to go off. "Don't worry, we'll get it taken care of."

"Oh, I'm not worried about that," Mrs. Darling says with a wave of her hand and a peel of laughter. "I was just worried about y'all. Everybody okay?"

"We're just fine, thanks," Royal says.

"That's good," she says. "I can't imagine how I'd feel if my Devlin got in an accident. Good thing he's such a safe driver. You can't be too careful, especially with a car like that."

Forgetting my manners, I gape at the lunatic. Okay, so I'm starting to see why he might have dated Redneck Barbie. His mom is a suburban housewife version, and I'd bet money her medicine cabinet could rival Mom's.

"Need me to lend you a hand?" Devlin asks, smirking at us. "It's not far. We can probably just push her up your driveway."

"We got it," Royal says, glaring daggers at our smug neighbor.

"Nonsense," Mrs. Darling coos. "My Devlin's happy to help, aren't you, baby? He's strong, too. But I bet you can see that."

She laughs and bats at his arm in a way that's just bordering on flirtatious.

Devlin works his jaw back and forth.

"Let me just hop in there and steer," Mrs. Darling says, skirting around the Range Rover toward the driver's seat.

"We don't need to push it," King says. "I'll just park it at the end of our drive."

The engine's running, so he can steer us out of the ditch, but we'll need new tires before we drive anywhere on those rims.

"Oh, boy," Mrs. Darling says, bending over slowly to pick up a nail in the road. "Would you look at this? No wonder you got a flat."

"Three flats," Royal mutters, glaring at Devlin.

Devlin gazes back impassively.

"Some kids must have been playing out here," Mrs. Darling says. "I'll have to talk to the neighborhood watch about this. Imagine! Nails in the road. It's a blessing y'all were going so slow. It could have been a real tragedy."

I stare hard at Devlin, waiting for the slightest twitch to give him away, but he only watches, his expression serene, the afternoon sun gleaming on his golden hair like he's every inch the angel his mother believes he is.

Royal circles the front of the car and cuts off Mrs. Darling, sliding into the driver's seat. There's no way he's going to let this nutcase, or anyone else, drive his car. He pulls forward, bouncing over a few loose bricks and lumbering back onto the road. As he pulls off the road into our driveway, Mrs. Darling stares after him, absently smoothing her hands over her middle. I don't miss the way she's sucking in her belly and poking out her boobs, though.

"I've been meaning to pop by and say hello to your daddy all week, and this gives me just the excuse," she says, turning and whisking the pie from my hands before beaming up at King. "I remember him from high school. He was quite the looker back then, just like you boys."

Oh, god. I turn away to roll my eyes, only to be caught by Devlin Darling. Shit.

"You know you're going to pay for this," I mutter to him.

"For what?" he asks, his expression a complete blank, as if he has no idea what I'm talking about.

"You're fucking with the wrong family," I tell him. "And please keep your drunk mother away from my dad."

His brows draw together and his lips tighten. At last, a reaction.

"I could say the same thing," he grinds out. "Keep your lecherous dad away from my mother."

"Well," I say, adjusting my ponytail over my shoulder. "I guess that's one thing we can agree on. Our families don't mix."

"Deal."

Royal has returned from his car, and he frowns when he sees me talking to Devlin. "Come on, Crys," he says, tucking a protective arm around me and steering me away.

We all start up our driveway, Mrs. Darling's pink-clad ass twitching with every step as she marches in front. Curious to see if Devlin's following, I glance back over my shoulder. I can't help myself.

He watches us go with cool detachment, as if he's above it all. Standing alone in the road, his shoulders straight and broad, his head held high, he looks every inch royalty. More than royalty. The sun lights him up like a golden god.

He doesn't take a single step in our direction, but he doesn't walk away, either. Something inside me pulls tight when I see him standing there alone. I wonder if under that chiseled stone exterior, he aches to join us. He knows he can't fraternize with the enemy, though. I remember what it's like to be on top, to know you can't join others because it means vacating your throne. If you do that for even a minute, someone else might take it. My brothers are lined up to take Devlin's right now.

As I tear my eyes from Devlin, I can't help thinking, I'm more like him than he knows—more than I'll ever let him know. I know the fear, how it eats you up. It's lonely at the top, even for an unsmiling, cruel god.

ten

I walk into my room an hour later and nearly scream with shock.

"What the hell are you doing here?" I whisper, shoving the door closed quickly, instinctively. I don't know why I'm hiding Devlin, or why he's here, or why I know my brothers can't see this, except that I don't want them to go to prison for murder.

"About time," Devlin says, sitting up and swinging his legs off the side of my bed, where he was reclining on the pillows like a king. "I've been waiting for an hour."

"Why are you in my room?" I whisper-shout, gesturing to the door. "My brothers are going to straight murder you."

He looks less than concerned. "How many pillows does one bed need?" he asks, tossing one of my pillows into the air and catching it. "I mean, even if you want to sleep upright, you've got more than enough. What do you use all these for?"

"Give me that," I hiss, snatching for the lavender silk accent pillow.

He tucks it under his arm and leans over on his elbow, trapping it under him and grinning up at me. "And aren't you supposedly in the mafia? You should be used to finding strange things in your bed, right? It's better than a horse's head."

"How did you even get in here?" I demand.

"You should really think about locking your window," he says, gesturing lazily to my window, where the curtains sway gently in the breeze. He removed the screen, leaving the window open onto the balcony. He must have climbed the outside staircase while we were all inside, which is pretty goddamn ballsy of him.

"You need to leave," I say, my heart hammering in my ears. It takes everything I've got not to shrink back against the door. He came into my room and waited an hour for me, maybe went through my things. What kind of psycho does that?

"First, tell me what they're talking about," he says.

"Who?"

"Our parents," he says, as if I should know.

"I don't know," I say, throwing my hands up. "Nothing. Boring shit."

"Like what?" Devlin asks, his eyes hardening.

I sigh. "They're reminiscing about high school."

"I thought I told you to keep your dad away from my mom," he says through clenched teeth. "In fact, keep your whole family away from mine. I don't know who you think you are coming in here and fucking with us, but if you don't stop, you're going to regret it."

"She's the one in our house," I pointed out. "You're the one who climbed in my window. I think *you're* the family that needs to stay away from ours."

"Your dad tried this shit before," Devlin says. "It didn't work then, and it won't work now. Keep him away from us."

"What are you talking about?"

He stares at me for a long minute, as if he doesn't believe I don't know this. His shades are pushed up on top of his head, and suddenly, I wish they weren't. I don't want to see his eyes, don't want to see the way they see right through me, through all my defenses. I've never been alone with him, and I suddenly, it feels terribly dangerous.

Devlin's lips curl into a cruel smirk, and I know for sure that he saw into me.

"Are you afraid of me, Crystalline?" he asks, springing up from the bed and crossing my room in three strides.

"No," I say, backing up a step.

He fills the space. His presence fills my whole room, sucks up all the air and leaves me breathless. He backs me against the door, his neck arching to look down at me, his fingers curling around my throat in a hold that's just barely more than a caress, just barely less than a threat.

"You should be," he whispers, the corners of his mouth curving into that sadistic smile.

"Well, I'm not." My pulse flutters against his fingertips but I won't give in that easily. I grip his wrist to pull it away, but the harder I pull to remove it from my throat, the harder he squeezes.

"Let tonight be a warning," he says. "Stay the fuck away from my family. Be the good dog I know you can. Because if you don't, I will make your life a living nightmare. I will make you wish you weren't alive at all." He strokes my cheek gently with his free hand, lifting my chin with his other. "I will strip you bare, and I'll make you beg for me even though you know I'll break you so good you'll be begging me to stop. But I won't stop. I will break you piece by piece until there's nothing left of you but sugar crystals, my sweet."

He strokes my lower lip, and a rush of tingles sweeps over my skin even as he holds me pinned to the door. He steps forward, until there's only a whisper of space between our bodies, a gulf that's charged with a hot electricity that races through my whole body. I inhale the scent of him, like freshly mown grass with a hint of leather and the intoxicating, dizzying aroma of boy sweat. I want to be grossed out, but I nearly swoon when I inhale him.

"You're sick," I whisper, my fingers shaking as I squeeze his wrist, my nails biting into his skin.

"Oh, sweetheart," he murmurs, his lips so close to mine I'm not sure if the heat I feel is his skin or just his breath. "You have no idea."

I squeeze harder, my nails sinking so deep they break the thin skin on the inside of his wrist. He sucks in a breath, and his eyes flash with something unreadable, something I take as anger.

"You made me bleed," he growls. "You shouldn't have done that."

"I—I'm sorry." I cringe backwards, but when Devlin's gaze fixes on my lips, I realize he's not pissed. His eyes are clouded with lust. My own body responds, my thighs hot even though every part of my brain is screaming for me to run.

"Disobey me, little mongrel," he purrs. "I dare you. I'll enjoy watching you shatter."

His lips brush over mine, a touch as light as the flutter of a butterflies wing, and a hot shiver of pleasure ripples through my traitorous body. My eyelids fall closed, and I tilt my head up before I have time to think.

His response is a cruel chuckle. "Oh, no," he says, stepping back to put distance between our bodies. My eyes fly open, and shame burns through me. Devlin's hand still grips my jaw, and triumph lights his eyes. "That's all you get, little dog. Now run and tell your brothers they're fucking with the wrong people. No one can replace the Darlings in this town. You can take my word for it, or you can learn the hard way."

He turns on his heel and is out the window in three seconds flat. I hear his soft footsteps on the balcony as I sink down against the inside of my door, closing my eyes and trying to catch my breath. My heart has been racing for so long I feel sick, and my limbs are shaking. And oh god, I hate myself for falling into his trap so easily. I hate my heart for pounding when he's near; I hate the butterflies that swarm in my belly until I'm dizzy when I catch a trace of his scent. I hate that when I look into his eyes, I see more than a privileged, arrogant asshole. I see someone who's more than he lets people know, someone who bleeds and hurts like the rest of us.

When I look into his eyes, I don't just see a monster. I see myself.

eleven

They must have a weakness. That's what my brother says. It's a house of cards. Take one out, and the whole thing folds. We just have to figure out what it is before they figure out our weakness.

The problem is, I think it's too late. Devlin already knows the Dolces' weakness.

Me.

The next day, we arrive to find the Bel Air in our parking space, the one Daddy's big donation bought us. "Is he really going to fuck with us after he wrecked my car?" Royal fumes.

Devlin's words the night before play through my mind, and I grab his arm. "Just leave it," I plead with my brother. "It doesn't matter. It's a parking space, for fuck's sake. Are you really going to get suspended over something so stupid? Come on. Just park somewhere else and ignore them."

Royal's nostrils flare as he glares at the shiny, powder-blue classic convertible in his spot. I have to admit, it's a really nice car. Considering the shape the Range Rover's in after last night, I don't blame Royal for being pissed to see it sitting there in his spot, rubbing salt in the wound. Still, I don't want my brothers anywhere near the Darlings. I'd rather just make peace and move on.

"We'll deal with him later," King says to Royal, pulling into another parking space. I relax just a bit, hoping that my brothers can see how petty and ridiculous it is to fight over one parking spot when the rest of the lot's wide open.

The Darling's sit on their car, like usual. Dolly is standing against her pink Barbie pickup with another girl, both of them watching the Darlings while talking, obviously pretending they're not watching the boys. As we approach, they stop pretending and watch us openly, like everyone else who's still hanging around the lot.

"Back where you belong today," Devlin drawls with a bored smirk on his lips. Lips that make butterflies explode inside me when I look at them.

Damn it.

"Ignore him," I hiss, grabbing Royal's arm and squeezing.

"Out back by the Dumpsters," Preston adds over the head of a girl who's wrapped around him like some kind of parasitic vine.

Devlin told me to leave his family alone, but apparently that doesn't go both ways.

And then his words from last night echo through my head. "I dare you…"

Is he goading my brothers, hoping we'll react so he can take it out on me? This has nothing to do with me. I shouldn't even be walking in with my brothers. If I separate myself from them at school, the Darlings will have to see that I'm not part of this little game they have going.

"I'm going to find Dixie," I tell my brothers. "I'll find you guys later."

I hurry away, leaving them to figure out the parking issue with the Darlings. I'm not going to get caught up in this ridiculous power struggle over a parking space. I want nothing to do with it, especially until my heart stops flopping like a fish every time I hear Devlin's name, or see his smile, or remember the smell of his skin as he leaned close…

I do a great job of avoiding Devlin first period, but when I arrive in lit, Colt pats the seat beside him. He sits sprawled in his chair, his legs out in the aisle like a desk can't contain him. "Sit, Sugar," he says with a big, easy grin.

"I can't," I say with a tight smile.

"Your brothers have you on a short leash," he says, still grinning like it doesn't matter. But I hear an edge of challenge in his voice, a tone that scares me more than Devlin's heart-stopping glare. Because as much as Devlin intimidates me, Colt tempts me. He tempts me to do something reckless, something deadly.

"It's not my brothers," I say. "It's your cousin."

Turning, I hurry to an empty desk. Just as I'm about to sit, Colt slips into the seat.

"Seat's taken." He grins up at me, that challenge still there, growing stronger now. I stare back at him, not moving. The truth is, I want to accept that challenge. I want to step over the line, do something wild and dangerous. I want to defy Devlin, to prove he doesn't scare me, even though he does. To show myself, if I can't show him, that he doesn't control my life.

But that would be asking for it.

"What are you doing?" I demand of Colt.

"Seat's taken," he says again, leaning forward and bracing a forearm on the desk. Hard, ropy muscle threads along his arm, fine threads of golden hair shining against his tan skin.

"Fine." I sigh and move to sit down in the next row, but he slips around the back of his seat and drops into the one I'm aiming for. By now, we've drawn the attention of a few people. They all watch, waiting for something.

Maybe the signal to start barking at me.

Fuck. I'd better bore them before that happens.

"What do you want?" I hiss at Colt, gritting my teeth and trying not to look around at the expectant faces in the class.

He pats the seat beside him. "You can sit here."

"I'm not sitting beside you."

"Okay." He smiles up at me, but it doesn't reach his eyes. Despite the lazy, stoner vibe he puts off, there's something calculating and hard in his gaze. He won't give up, I realize. Not until I obey.

And really, what will it hurt? This is silly—running around the class playing some stupid game of musical chairs. I can just sit where I did yesterday and ignore Colt. I spin, flicking my hair over my shoulder at him, and march over to the empty seat. I drop into it before he can reach it. I'm being as immature as he is. I could have just sat beside him where he is. But if the only power I have is to make him come to me, that's what I'll do.

A second later, he slides in next to me. "Hey, Sugar," he says. "Glad you came around to my way of thinking."

The relaxed, easy grin belies the iron will I saw behind those grey eyes a second ago. But I won't forget it's there.

"What do you want?" I whisper, leaning low and turning my head toward him so prying eyes can't decipher my words.

"Can't a hot guy want to talk to a pretty girl?" he asks, seemingly oblivious to my irritation.

"Not when their families want to kill each other."

"You want to kill me?" he asks with feigned surprise.

I grit my teeth. "Right now?"

121

Colt laughs, a big easy laugh. He may look no more harmful than a big, friendly golden retriever, but I saw the determination in his eyes. I know there's more to this guy than meets the eye.

If he's going to play that game, then I'll play along. I don't know his reasons, but if he doesn't want people to know he's more than a laid-back flirt, who am I to blow his cover? I know all about hiding behind a facade, about having to be a certain way because that's what people want and expect. And I know that if he wanted to share more with me, he would have done it instead of deflecting with a flirtatious comment.

So, I let it go. When he nudges me during class, I look down to see a sheet of paper edging onto my desk, his lazy scrawl covering multiple lines.

If our families want to kill each other, we could def be Romeo and Juliet.

I can't help but smile. I want to be mad at him for manipulating me into sitting with him, but I can't. Even if I don't know his reasons, and I don't trust him, that doesn't mean I have to spend the whole class being miserable or angry. I can keep my guard up and still have a little fun flirting with a cute boy. It's not like I ever got to do that back home.

Hm, I don't like our chances.

I push the paper back to him. He cracks a smile and leans over the paper to scribble an answer. I try not to admire the broadness of his shoulders, the plane of his back as he bends to write.

If you don't want to die young, we'll rewrite the ending.

I snort and send back a quick response. *You can't rewrite the end of R&J. That's what makes the story.*

He scoots down in his desk and squints at the teacher for a minute, seeming to think. Then he smiles to himself, straightens, and begins to write. I find my heartbeat picking up just a bit, anticipation building as he formulates his answer. I watch the smile twitching at the corner of his lips, and I find myself holding back a goofy grin of my own. The high of flirting with him is heady and intoxicating. A dangerous thrill goes through me when I realize my brothers won't know. No one at this school is going to run and tell them if a guy is flirting with me. Especially not a Darling.

But his cousins might know. He might tell them.

The thought sends a shot of adrenaline charging through me. Half of me is terrified he'll tell Devlin. The other half thrills at the thought of what he'll do if I disobey him. Will he come through my window again, shove me up against the door? Will he do more than threaten this time?

My heart is hammering, and I feel my face flush at the image.

Stupid heart. Stupid body. Stupid imagination.

Colt folds the paper in fourths and slides is back, pushing it under my hand. His fingers brush my skin and linger until I look up and meet his eye. He winks and retracts his hand.

We'll write our own story. We can call it Homey-O and Drooliet. *Totally fitting right?*

I roll my eyes. *Let me guess. Because you've all decided I'm a dog.*

No. Because you drool a little every time you see these guns.

When I snort with laughter and look up from reading that gem, Colt is leaning his elbow on his desk. He flexes and strokes the bulge of his bicep sensually.

This time, I can't help but laugh out loud. The teacher shoots me an irritated glare. "Mind joining us, Miss Dolce?"

"Yes, sorry," I mutter.

Colt lounges back in his chair, a gloating grin on his face. I slowly crumple up the paper we've been writing on, watching his face as I do it. A flicker of something passes through his gaze even as his smile remains firmly in place. It's gone so fast I can't tell if it was anger, insult, or interest.

I manage to ignore him for the rest of class, but my curiosity is piqued. I can't stop thinking about him. Wanting to know more about this boy who smiles so casually, so easily. The twins are the same way, flirty and fun, but there's something more about Colt. Something darker under that sunshiny surface.

I make it through the rest of class, and then through the rest of the day. At home, I tell my brothers that maybe we should just leave the Darlings alone. We had our time at the top. If they really need it again, maybe we can make a truce with the Darlings.

Royal laughs at that. They wrecked his car. He's never going to forgive them. Royal is my rock. He's loyal and protective and good. But forgiveness is not a word in his vocabulary.

Still, he promises that if he cooks up any revenge schemes, I'll be far away when he enacts them. Whatever they do, I won't be involved in any way. The Darlings can take it up with my brothers and leave me out of it. My brothers are suspiciously quiet after that, and I don't pry. I don't want to know what they're up to. Ignorance is bliss and all that. If I don't know, I can't be held accountable for anything they do.

At school the next week, I hang out with Dixie, giving her tips on makeup, boys, and fashion. I settle into my classes. A few subdued woofs and snickers are the only indication that people remember the first day of school. No one gangs up to bark at me, and the Darlings pretty much leave me alone, except Colt, who forces me to sit with him in lit. Devlin doesn't come storming into my bedroom, so I guess Colt is keeping his mouth shut.

Every day, we leave the house ridiculously early so we can arrive at school and park in the primo spot before the Darlings get there. At home I study, ignore the midnight football noises from next door, and keep an eye on Daddy to make sure he's not thinking of entertaining Mrs. Darling again. The first weekend passes quietly. Too quietly. I'm starting to get nervous about my brothers. Since the mailbox incident, we've been taking two cars to work—King's Evija and Duke's Hummer. The Range Rover sits in the garage with new tires, but with the side all bashed in, reminding me every day that retaliation is brewing.

The next Friday morning, even though we arrive early, the Bel Air is parked in our spot again. My brothers don't say a word, which makes my blood run cold. I know better than to think they've stopped fighting. My brothers will never stop. Once they get something in their heads, it's impossible to convince them of anything else. Even I can't persuade them, and they'd do anything for me.

Royal walks me to my first class, but he keeps glancing around as if distracted. As if waiting for something.

"What's up?" I ask. It's not like my fight-happy brother to be jumpy.

"Nothing," he says. "But maybe you should stay home tonight."

I swallow hard and nod. As much as I want to go to the game and scope out the competition with my brothers, if they're brawling tonight, I don't want to be part of it. Staying home from the game altogether is the clearest way to let the Darlings know that even if I'm loyal to my family, I'm not on board with the escalating pranks. I've survived two weeks at Willow Heights, but every moment of this dance has been done on eggshells.

The bell rings, and I wave and head to first period, grateful to see that Devlin's absent. He seems to only attend first period when he feels like it, which is about half the time. I'm not complaining. I slide in at our lab table and let out a breath. I'm not sure how to explain my feelings about Devlin even to myself. When I sit next to him in class, it's hard to breathe. My body is electric when he's near, my skin aching to move closer, to press against his. But as soon as he speaks, I want to punch him in the nuts. I hear him throwing the football at night, and I'm drawn to my balcony, hoping each night I'll catch a glimpse of him as I did that first time. And then he smiles that cold, dangerous smile that makes him as terrifying and hypnotic as a snake.

I shake my thoughts away and try to focus. Nothing about Devlin Darling fits into my plan to be better here. Nothing about him would fit into my life, not with my brothers at war with him. Still, he hasn't moved seats or asked me to move since the first day we sat together. Sometimes, I catch him looking at me, and for a second I can see the real Devlin, see into him, see that he's just human like the rest of us. Sometimes, he even makes me laugh with his quiet, unexpected humor. And then he makes some rude, bossy comment that shows what an entitled prick he really is.

After class I head to my locker, hoping I'll get lucky and find Colt missing from second period. I notice a few people whispering as I stop at my locker, but I can't tell if it's worse than usual. I am the Darling Dog, after all. And though nothing has really come of it, I get just enough comments and dog noises to know no one has forgotten. It hangs over me, following me like an echo through the halls. I can't forget for a moment that I've been marked.

I start to twist the combination lock when I smell something familiar that I can't place, a smell that's half stale grease, a quarter musty, and a quarter something else. I slow as I click the lock around to the second number, but my mind is racing. I can turn around and demand to know who did it, even though I'm not exactly sure what "it" is. I can hurry to class without opening my locker, but if I do that, everyone will know I'm running away. Or I can open my locker and face whatever they put in here.

I've done plenty of running, hiding, and pretending, but I prefer to do it when I won't look like I'm running scared. Being a Dolce means never losing face, and if that means letting them laugh at me, I'll do it. If I don't lose my cool, I can keep my dignity even in the face of their laughter. And if I don't react, they'll lose interest soon enough.

Taking a deep breath, I stop at the last number, feeling the lock catch before it gives. The second the latch gives, the door jumps open as if on a spring. I jump back involuntarily, even though I thought I was ready for it. The door swings open, and a cascade of dogfood pellets flood out of my locker. They rain down on the floor, scattering across the hall, burying the toes of my nude pumps.

A few people bark, but most of them just laugh. I stare at my locker, my heart pounding, my mind racing.

Don't react, I tell myself. *Take your books, close your locker, and go to class like nothing happened. Whatever you do, don't shed a tear, no matter what else they do.*

I reach forward and pull out my Shakespeare book, my hands trembling, my fingers numb. More dogfood rains down from in front of and on top of my books. I reach for my locker door, willing myself not to cry. I won't give them the satisfaction.

Before I can shut my locker, a hand grabs the door from behind and slams it shut with a metallic bang that echoes down the hall. Devlin is standing behind it, his palm flat against my closed locker, his eyes blazing into mine. A titter of nervous laughter makes its way through the hall, and I search for my brothers, thinking someone saw them coming.

But they're nowhere to be seen. These people aren't afraid of my brothers, or of seeing a fight. They're afraid of Devlin.

Seeing the fury crackling in his icy eyes, it's easy to see why he inspires fear. I just don't know why anyone but me should be afraid.

"Who did this?" Devlin asks, turning slowly to face the crowd.

A murmur goes through the gathering crowd, but no one steps up. I'd assumed he did it, and if not him, one of his cousins. But he looks like he's about to fly off the handle. I don't get it. He designated me the Darling Dog. He painted a target on me. And now he's pissed that someone targeted me?

"What's going on here?" calls an exasperated teacher's voice, and a petite older teacher in a pencil skirt and blazer pushes through the crowd.

"Go away," Devlin says, not even looking at her. "This is Darling business. It doesn't concern you."

She looks like she's going to argue, but then she pinches her lips together and glares with disapproval. Without another word, she turns and pushes back through the crowd, leaving me gaping. Fuck. The Darlings aren't even a little bit afraid of consequences, because for them, there are none. If I had any doubts that they run this school, they're gone now. So is any chance at getting out of the scene unfolding around me.

And as much as I want to run away with that teacher, some insatiably curious part of me is dying to know what comes next, even though I know it can't be good. I am fascinated by Devlin's rage. Like a storm-chaser, I want to follow, to witness his destructive power even though I know this storm could wreck me.

I know he wouldn't let me go, anyway. And when Colt slips up to my other side, the game is over. They'll stop me if I try to run now.

"This is the Darling Dog," Devlin says to the crowd, his hand shooting out and grabbing me by the back of my neck. He pulls me to his side, but this time, there's no violence in his grip. It's firm and possessive, not cruel. "She's *my* dog. Understand?"

"Make her eat it," a guy calls, then shrinks back when Devlin swings his gaze in that direction.

"Who said that?" Devlin asks, his grip tightening.

Devlin's gaze bores into the crowd, and after a few seconds, the guy who spoke gives a nervous laugh. "I just thought it would be funny."

"Is this a joke to you?" Devlin demands.

"Well—"

Before he can finish, Devlin cuts him off. "This isn't about pranks. This is real. This girl is a dog. *Our* dog. No one feeds her, or takes her for rides, or pets her without our permission."

"Sorry," the guy says, shuffling back a step.

"You can eat it, since you think it's funny," Preston says, stepping through the crowd. Of all the Darlings, I know him least, and yet, he's just as scary. His threats sound like jokes, but from the spark of mean in his eyes, I get the feeling he'd love to enact every sick threat he makes.

"What?" asks the unfortunate guy who spoke, his eyes going wide when he sees that all three Darling cousins are here.

Preston speaks slowly. "Pick up a handful, and eat it."

The guy glances from one side to the other, as if searching for someone to rescue him. But the teachers are obviously not going to interfere in this ritual. After a second, the guy bends and scoops up a handful. His face reddens with humiliation as he brings it to his mouth, but he doesn't stop. He puts the pellets in his mouth and begins to chew.

"Who fed our dog?" Devlin demands, not even bothering to watch the public shaming his cousin ordered. No one answers, but a group of popular girls laugh nervously.

"You?" he asks, his gaze fixed on them with maliciousness that makes me scared for them. Yeah, they pulled a shitty prank to humiliate me, but I have a feeling they're about to get something a lot worse than a locker full of dogfood.

"It was just a joke," Lacey says at last.

"Am I laughing?" Devlin asks, his voice quiet but thunderous. His fingers are shaking with barely contained fury, and it strikes me how completely unhinged this guy is. If he looked crazy when he was holding me by the throat, all cool and calculating, now he looks… Straight psycho, batshit crazy, insane. I'm suddenly afraid for Lacey. True, she's a bitch, but even bitches have dignity.

"It's not that big a deal," I say quickly.

"Quiet," Devlin orders, giving me a little shake. Staring at Lacey and her friends, he holds out his other hand. "Give me your dolls."

What. The. Actual. Fuck.

"What? No," Lacey cries, her eyes going wide and her fingers flying to her throat.

"We didn't mean anything by it," another girl says, sounding close to tears. She shoots me a look of sheer panic, as if I can save her from the fate she chose.

"You're not worthy of Dolly's legacy," Devlin says.

"It was Lacey's idea," whines another girl.

"And you went along with it," Colt says. "You really shouldn't have fucked with our puppy."

Devlin narrows his eyes at the girl. "You're weak. Not one of you deserves to be a Doll."

"I'm sorry," the girl whimpers, tears pooling in her eyes as she pulls a necklace from inside her shirt. A tiny crystal ballerina hangs on the silver chain. Her hand is visibly shaking as she drops it into Devlin's outstretched palm. She shoots me one withering, hateful look before wiping her tears.

"I left mine at home," says another girl, her voice trembling.

"Go get it," Devlin says. "Until you get back, your friends will be feasting."

"What?" Lacey asks, looking horrified. "I can't dogfood. I'm a Darling Doll!"

"Not anymore," Devlin says, a sadistic spark of triumph in his eyes as he wraps his hand around the three ballerina pendants.

"But... I'm gluten free," she protests.

"On your hands and knees," Devlin says slowly, a cruel smile twisting his lips. "All three of you will eat like dogs until she gets back."

"Hurry," says another girl, and the one who left her necklace at home turns and sprints down the hall toward the exit.

Preston's hand lazily moves to his crotch, giving himself a stroke through his slacks. "I've got something else you can do on your knees if you'd rather."

"No," Devlin snaps. "They'll clean up the mess they made."

I feel sick as I watch the three girls sink to their knees in the dogfood kernels. I must not be alone, as there is no more laughter. The hall is silent as we watch Lacey put a single pellet between her trembling lips and begin to chew.

"That's not how dogs eat," Preston says, holding up his phone to film the scene. "Get your ass in the air and pick it up off the floor with those pretty lips you like to use so much."

For a moment, Lacey's eyes catch on me, and she glares at me with such intense hatred I shrink back. With a hiccupping breath, she lowers her mouth to the floor and gets a kernel between her lips. As she chews, the crunch echoes through the silence, and a tear trickles down her cheek. She sniffs and picks up another piece, more tears coming now. The other girls are crying, too, all of them silently eating the dogfood they filled my locker with as a hateful, ugly prank.

I can't help but feel horrified at the pitiful sight of them eating dogfood off the floor. I don't like bullies, but I don't like this, either.

"I think that's enough," I say. "You've proved your point."

Devlin spins around, pinning me to the lockers with his body. He leans on the metal with both elbows, caging me in. My breath comes faster as our bodies make contact, a contact that feels dangerously good in this bizarre situation, as if he's somehow a comfort instead of a threat.

"You've completely missed the point," he growls. "I say when it's enough. What I say goes in this school. Not you, and not your city-boy brothers. Me."

His eyes blaze into mine, and I nod, instinctively darting my tongue out to wet my lips. The movement catches Devlin's eye, and he drops his gaze to my lips for a long moment, one that wakes butterflies inside my belly.

No, no, no...

"Be a good dog, and obey your master," he says, so softly that only me and Colt, who's standing next to us, can hear. "Now, go to class before you get yourself into any more trouble."

twelve

The guys go to the game that night, but Daddy bribes me to stay home with the promise that we'll spend some time together. When the guys leave, he's still not home. A storm brews on the horizon, and the heat has finally broken for the time being. I sit out on the balcony wrapped in a robe, watching lightning flicker in the distance. Where is he?

My phone rings, startling me. A jolt of fear shoots through me as I fumble it from my robe, sure I'll see Daddy calling to say he was in an accident, or worse, that my brothers did something stupid.

Instead, I see a video chat request from Mom. "Darling," she says when I accept the call. "Don't frown like that. I don't want to pay to smooth out those wrinkles until you're at least twenty."

"Hi, Mom," I say, rolling my eyes. "How's everything back home?"

She makes a face, and I consider hassling her about wrinkles, but I decide to keep my pettiness to myself for now. She's here for me right now when no one else is, and the call is a good distraction from my melancholy thoughts and groundless worries.

"You know, I thought it would be a lot more exciting than it's been," she says. "It turns out, life as a single gal isn't so glamourous. It's no different than when you were here, except I have no one to talk to when I get bored."

"Glad we could entertain you all those years."

"Where's your father?"

"Working," I say. "Of course."

She pouts at me. "You know, he might have been a good husband if he weren't already married to his job. No woman wants to be the mistress in her own marriage."

"Problems for your therapist, Mom." Not to mention that without Daddy's job, Mom never would have been able to maintain the life she loves so much in Manhattan.

She starts telling me a long story about something scandalous she found out about her therapist. I half listen, thankful for the distraction of her endless gossip. I don't care who her married therapist is banging, but the familiarity of her gossiping is comforting.

When she finally finishes her story, dark has fallen. Still no sign of Daddy. The Darling house sits dark and empty next door, the whole family undoubtedly off at the game. Apparently, football is a family affair in the south.

That reminds me of Daddy's earlier confession. "Did you know that Daddy grew up around here?" I ask Mom.

She sighs and rolls her eyes. "He didn't grow up there. He went to school there for a few years in high school, and he likes to pretend that makes him belong there. You all belong in New York as much as I do. When is he going to get that silly idea out of his head and move back?"

"You want him back?" I ask, a lump forming in my throat.

"He's the one who left me," she says. "You all left me."

I shake my head, refusing to be deterred. "So, that's why he wanted to build a branch here? Because he went to high school here."

She sighs again. "I assume so."

"Did he ever talk about a family called the Darlings?" I ask. "That he knew back then?"

"Oh, I don't know," she says. "He talked about it sometimes, but it all sounded so deathly boring."

"You've heard of them?" I ask. "Their son said Dad had tried to mess with them before."

"Your father is a businessman," Mom says. "Sometimes in a business, you have to make tough decisions."

"So, it was business," I say. "Not personal."

I have to admit, I'm relieved. I was afraid it was something more scandalous, like an affair. Even though I get along better with Daddy than I do with Mom, I'd be devastated for her if he'd messed around.

"Yes," Mom said with a sniff. "What else? With your father, it's always business."

"What did he do?" Lightning flickers on the horizon, and I glance at the driveway again, wondering where he is now. She's right, though. Work always comes first. He probably forgot about our plans and stayed late at the office again.

"Who knows," Mom says. "I think that Darling guy claimed that *Dolce Drops* were his idea. Which is ridiculous, of course. If they were his idea, they'd be *Darling Drops.*"

Some old business grudge, then. Nothing sensational at all. In fact, kind of a letdown. Not that I want drama between our families, but the Darlings obviously did fine for themselves without any help from Daddy. What I can't figure out is why he wanted to move in right next door to a man who accused him of stealing his patent or whatever.

"Not everyone can win, Crystal," Mom says, sipping her martini and checking her image in the corner of the screen. "There will always be losers. You have to accept that reality and not get caught up in the fate of the losers. You have to take care of yourself. We always tried to teach you kids that."

"You did a great job," I say. Mom always looks out for number one, that's for sure.

"Good," she says. "Dolce's always win. Don't forget that."

"I won't," I say, glancing at the Darling house. I wonder if they tell Devlin that. If they preach to him about being a winner, about looking good and strong, about never showing the cracks in his armor. I wonder if he has a family motto, if he feels five times the pressure I do because he's the only kid, the heir to their family name and fortune.

I wonder if there's a way for the Dolces and the Darlings to both win. Right now, it doesn't look like it.

thirteen

Who picks a girl to treat like a dog for the entire school year? Monsters, that's who. Sick fucks. Sociopaths. If some part of me understands them, or wants to understand them, does that make me a sociopath, too?

On Monday, Royal pulls the Range Rover out of the garage and sits idling in the driveway while the rest of my brothers pile in. He hasn't driven the car since the accident, and with good reason. It looks like a beater car.

"What are you doing?" I ask, peering suspiciously at the dented and scraped vehicle. One of the headlights is smashed, along with the side panel behind it, the passenger side door, and part of the rear door behind it.

"Driving to school," Royal says. "Duke, take Crystal in your car."

"No way," Duke says. "I'm not missing the look on those assholes faces when we show up."

"Why do I feel like you're going to get arrested?" I ask.

"Because you worry too much," Duke says, throwing an arm around me. "Now come on, if we follow right behind them, we'll get to see it all go down."

"Whatever's going down, I don't want to see it," I say. But I get in the car with Duke, anyway. Maybe some part of me is still the nosy bitch I was in New York. Or maybe I just want to know what my brothers are doing. It's definitely not because I want to see the Darlings, too, because I can't help but be drawn to them like a voyeur looking in at their lives, trying to figure them out. Or so I tell myself.

I climb in the Hummer with Duke and Baron, and we follow the smaller car like a military escort. It sends a message for sure.

"Is this your way of telling the school 'don't fuck with us, or we'll bring the big guns,'?" I ask.

Baron laughs from the passenger seat. "Sure."

"Those ass-wipes are going down," Duke sings, obviously high with the excitement of taking down the Darlings.

I remember Devlin's words, and stomach flips. "You're sure you can't just call it even and move on? I mean, would it really be so bad to have an even bigger crew? One that wasn't just our family. Think about it. There would be seven of you instead of four. You'd be almost twice as powerful."

"You really don't get how this works, do you?" Baron asks, twisting around to smile at me from behind his glasses. A dimple sinks into his cheek, and he's still my adorable little brother, no matter what scheme he's cooking up.

I open my mouth to tell him what Devlin said, but then I close it. If I tell my brothers that he threatened me, they'll do a lot worse than whatever they're planning as revenge for Royal's car. I'm not about to stick my nose in the middle of this and make things worse. I'm just going to stay far away from the whole thing, watch what goes down from the sidelines, and let the boys work things out on their own. It's not like they'd listen to me, anyway.

We pull into the parking lot early, as usual. During the past week, my brothers have played the stupid game with the Darlings where they each try to arrive earlier than the other so they can get the primo parking spot. But today, instead of cursing and glowering when the Darlings steal their spot, Baron cackles as he sets his phone on the dash in video mode. Duke pulls into the parking lot and circles around so we're a row behind the Bel Air. He stops in the middle of the road, ignoring a car that pulls up behind him, waiting to turn down a row of parking spaces.

"What are you doing?" I ask again, my heart hammering in my ears so loudly I can barely hear my own words. "Because whatever it is, you need to stop."

"I'm just capturing it on video," Baron says. "This is going to get so many hits on my YouTube channel."

I lean forward between the seats, anxiety churning inside me like a restless, storm-tossed sea. Royal cruises along the row of parking spaces in the Rover, not slowing as he moves toward his space. In fact, he seems to be speeding up. The dented door and broken light flash by, and I want to close my eyes, to cover them, but I can't. I stare in shock as the battered Rover shoots toward the Bel Air.

Devlin and Preston look up from their usual spot leaning against the car. And Colt... Annoyingly charming Colt is glued to his phone as always. A scream catches in my throat, and my hand flies out, as if I can stop Royal, as if I can grab Colt and yank him out of the way.

Preston yells something, leaping away from the car. Fear slaps across his face like a hand, erasing his perfect mask of indifference. Devlin grabs Colt and hauls him across the pavement, faster than he should be able to move with his cousin stumbling and protesting with confusion. And then the Range Rover barrels into the Bel Air like a wrecking ball.

A squeal of metal and smashing glass reverberates through the parking lot. The Bel Air skids out of its space, turning a full one-eighty as it bounces down the tiny strip of grass that separates the parking lot from the building and slides into the ditch, slamming to a stop against the end of a culvert.

Silence falls over the parking lot. Everyone is too stunned to move. Only a dozen people are outside, all of them standing frozen as they watch the beautiful chariot that carries the kings of the school turn into a crumpled heap, like a smashed tin can.

Devlin moves first. He leaps at the Rover, which sits sideways across the coveted parking spot. Steam billows up from the crumpled hood, the whole front end smashed in. I scream, lurching for the door of the Hummer and spilling out onto the pavement. I scramble to my feet as Devlin jerks open the crumpled passenger door. King jumps out to meet him, grabbing Devlin by the front of his jacket.

"Guess we didn't see you there," King growls, shaking Devlin. "In *our* parking space."

Devlin swings, his fist connecting with King's jaw. He's beyond words. His eyes are completely insane. Royal dives across the seat and leaps into the fight, smashing into Devlin and King. He goes for Devlin, who doesn't seem to care who he's punching. He slams a fist into Royal's face, smashing his nose. Royal stumbles back, reaching for Devlin, but he's too fast. He whirls like a dervish, fists raining down on my brothers. Blood sprays onto the pavement around them.

I scream and race toward them, blinded by panic. He's going to kill my brother.

There's no thought behind my urge to protect my twin, only instinct. Because if I could manage a thought, it would put me over the edge. If I could manage one thought, it would be that Devlin is completely insane. He fights with a recklessness that Royal doesn't have, with a complete lack of self-preservation, as if he doesn't care which one of them dies in this fight, but it's going to the death.

Before I reach them, Royal looks up from where he's throttling Devlin.

"Crystal, get the fuck away," he yells.

And in his one moment of distraction, Devlin strikes. His fist connects with Royal's head so hard I can hear the crack like a watermelon dropping to the ground. Royal crumples sideways, his body sprawling limp on the pavement.

I scream, diving for him. But Duke's strong arms wrap around me from behind, lifting me off my feet. I kick and scream, blinded by panic.

Devlin jumps to his feet and starts kicking Royal savagely, completely out of control and apparently unaware that Royal's no longer fighting.

"Stop," I scream, but no one is listening in the chaos. Everyone is screaming.

King tackles Devlin, and they crash to the ground. Preston leaps onto them, his arm wrapping around King's neck from behind. A second later, sirens blare in the lot, and a cop car jerks to a stop beside us. Two cops leap out and run over to break up the fight. Devlin's still going, punching so wildly I don't think he even knows that Preston's one of the people on him, or that a cop is. Only when they start beating the fighters with their clubs do they get them apart.

They push Devlin face down to the pavement and snap a pair of cuffs on his wrists. Preston and King stand with their hands above their heads, waiting their turn to be handcuffed.

"Who called the fucking cops?" Duke asks, his arms still around me as the cop arrests my oldest brother and two Darlings.

An ambulance arrives, and EMTs jump out and come over to pick up Royal. My heart nearly stops, and I tear myself free of Duke's grasp and run to my insane, fight-happy twin. All my brothers have their vices, their risky behaviors that make them feel alive, that put them so close to the edge that they can look over and stare death in the eyes. But Royal, my god. Why does he have to choose the most dangerous one of all?

I fall to my knees beside him, choking on a sob and ignoring the EMTs telling me to back off. He has to be okay. He fucking has to.

"Wake up," I beg him, gripping his hand like it's the only thing saving me from drowning. My voice drops to a whisper as tears stream down my face. "Please."

Royal's hand twitches a moment before his lids flutter open. His dark eyes lock on mine, and his fingers tighten. "Crystal."

"I'm here," I say, a hysterical laugh bubbling through my tears. "You big idiot. You were knocked out cold. You scared me to death."

"Everyone's okay?" he asks, struggling to sit up.

The EMTs push him back down, insisting he lie there while they get the stretcher ready.

"Fine," I say, wiping my face. "King and the Darlings got arrested."

Royal keeps saying he's okay, but they still want to put him in the ambulance, check if he has a concussion, and make a fuss over him. Devlin, Preston and King are sitting on curbs while the cops talk to a few students. The headmaster and some other admin are out now, urging us all to get to class. More cops arrive, as well as a wrecker to haul away the smashed cars.

I refuse to leave Royal's side. If he's going to the hospital, I'm sure as hell going with him. I don't want to give a statement about what happened. Baron has it all on video, anyway.

I accompany Royal to the hospital, where they tell him he has a concussion. Daddy comes in fuming mad, but after talking with Royal, he only nods and says, "Don't let anyone push you around, son."

Daddy drops us off at home that afternoon, leaves strict orders for me to take care of Royal, and goes off to deal with King. The house seems quiet without him. It's so big, bigger than the brownstone by at least three or four times. There are rooms in this place I don't even know the names for.

"I can't believe you did that," I say to Royal at last. "You could have gotten yourself killed."

"He had it coming," Royal says, laying back in a recliner. "He wrecked my car. I wrecked his."

"You might think you're even, but he won't," I point out. "What are you going to do? Just keep going until someone really does get killed?"

"I'm not going to let some asshole walk all over me," Royal says.

I sit down on the cushy leather arm of the recliner. "I know," I say with a sigh. That's not the Dolce way.

"Who called the cops?" Royal asks after a minute.

"I don't know," I say honestly. I wasn't exactly watching the crowd when it all went down.

"I guess it won't hurt us any," Royal says. "Them getting arrested. It might even make things easier on us."

I groan and close my eyes. This is never going to end. I realize that now. Until someone really does wind up dead, they're going to keep fighting. My brothers will never back down, and I have a feeling the Darlings are just as stubborn.

My phone is full of texts, so after Royal assures me he's fine and begs me to quit hovering, I go upstairs and pull my chair out onto the balcony. Most of the texts are from Dixie, freaking out and dying to know the gossip. I call her anyway.

"Oh my god, are you okay?" she asks in lieu of a hello.

"I'm fine," I say. "Royal's fine. Everyone's going to be okay."

"Did you see what happened to Devlin Darling's car?" she asks. "I don't think anything will be fine ever again!"

I laugh at that. "Don't you think that's a tad over dramatic?"

"That's not a car you can just go *buy*," she says. "Even if insurance replaces the cost, you can't replace that car."

"I'm sure someone fixes up old cars to sell," I say, my throat suddenly tight with nerves. I pick at a scab that's formed on my knee from this morning.

"He didn't buy that," Dixie said. "He and his dad built it. Like, from scratch!"

"Not from scratch," I say. "I mean, maybe they restored it, but it was already built."

"I'm just saying, it's irreplaceable. Devlin's going to be out for blood."

"What's the deal with his family?" I ask, studying the house where Devlin's pink-heeled mom and elusive dad live.

"His parents are divorced," she says. "From what I know, it was pretty messy. Both his parents are remarried."

I hear tires crunch on the gravel drive next door, and I look down to see Mr. Darling's car pulling into the garage around back. I can't tell if Devlin's in the passenger seat or not. He seemed pretty chummy with the woman who brought the pie, even calling her Mom. Now I wonder if the man of the house is not his dad after all.

"Which ones do we live next to?" I ask.

"His dad," she says. "His mom lives outside town somewhere. I don't know. It's not like I'm invited to their parties. Can you imagine, though?"

"Pretty sure all we'll ever do is imagine," I say. "Considering I'm a dog to them."

"Oh, sorry," she says. "I wasn't thinking. But you're right. You'll never get invited to a Darling party now."

"Bummer."

"I know," she says. "I hear they're, like, so epic. But like, scary, too. I heard that last year after homecoming, people were daring each other to do stuff, and some girl got dared to jump off the balcony into the pool. She broke her neck and died!"

"I'm sure that's just a rumor," I say automatically. I think of a dead girl, floating on top of a pool. I think of her parents finding her. I think of the messages they found on her phone, comments on her social media.

I squeeze my eyes closed and try to breathe.

Not a dead girl. She didn't die.

"No, it's true," Dixie insists. "Homecoming is this weekend. That's the anniversary. We should go see her grave. I know what cemetery she's buried in."

I shiver and wrap my arms around myself. I used to go to parties, but my brother kept me well guarded. Stuff happened, but it was more like someone got pregnant that night, or the twins switched out on a girl without telling her. Parties were fun. Not deadly.

"I won't be going to any afterparties next weekend," I tell Dixie.

"You have to go to the game, though," Dixie says as if it's a given.

"You're going?" I ask, surprised. I didn't peg Dixie for a football fan.

"Of course," she says, and I can practically hear her eyes rolling. "Everyone in town goes to homecoming. There's nothing else to do. Most of the stores even close. It would be a ghost town. It's bad enough during a regular game, but homecoming?"

"I don't know…"

"You're going," she says. "Everyone goes. It'll be fun. Besides, I know your brothers go. I saw them last week."

"You did?"

"Of course," she said. "I go to all the games. Everyone in school does."

"Not everyone," I mutter. From across the lawns between our houses, I hear the screen door of the Darling's house slam. A minute later, the familiar slap of the football hitting something starts up. He's early tonight. I usually don't hear Devlin practicing until late in the night.

"Your brothers might be at the game as players pretty soon," Dixie says. "I hear the Darlings might be off the team."

I sit up straight, my heart stopping in my chest. "What?"

"Well, I don't know about Preston and your brother," she says quickly. "But there's a video going around that clearly shows Devlin assaulting your brother, and then kicking him while he's passed out on the ground. It looks pretty bad, Crystal."

My head is spinning as it all falls into place. Baron wasn't just getting video so he can get hits on his YouTube channel. He set this all up. They knew exactly how much Devlin loved his car. His stepmom even said so the other day. They knew he'd lose his shit when they hit it. And knowing Baron, he spliced the video to show exactly what he wanted it to show. He's a wizard with video. He'd never admit it, but he's a total geek at heart. He might use football to hide it so he can still get laid, but the guy is a tech genius.

"You really think Devlin will be off the team?" I ask, my voice barely above a whisper. I shiver at the thought of how pissed he'll be, what he might do to retaliate if they take football away from him. I won't be sleeping with my window open anymore, that's for sure.

"I don't know," Dixie says. "His parents can probably get him back on. They can do anything in this town. But this time, it's not just the school. The cops were involved."

"The cops aren't in their pockets?" I ask, thinking of how much influence my dad had back home. Surely if my dad could make a NYPD cop look the other way, the Darlings can get a small-town cop to do the same.

"Depends on the cop," Dixie says. "Officer Gunn was one of the ones who arrested them, and he's definitely a good cop, but he's also friends with Mr. Darling." She breaks off and giggles. "He's cute, too. I'll point him out at the game on Friday."

I feel sick just thinking about the game. Yes, I want my brothers to have a chance with the coach, to be able to do the thing they do best. But I don't want to think about what Devlin might do to sabotage them after this. They didn't just wreck a car. They wrecked a priceless rebuilt classic that he worked on with his dad. They didn't just get him arrested. They recorded it, spliced it to make him look especially bad, and quite possibly got him kicked off the team for the rest of his senior year. If he loves football even half as much as my brothers, things are about to get even uglier.

fourteen

I know I did the right thing. Dixie is no longer the Darling Dog. She doesn't have to wear dog-ear headbands, and no one barks at her. If anyone's going to do something, they'll do it to me. And I can handle it. All I did was take away the bullies' victim. So why can't I rid myself of the little voice whispering in the back of my head that someone good, someone better, wouldn't ruin anyone, even if they deserved ruination, to get what they want?

"I don't know about this, Dixie," I say as we pull up at a cemetery in a part of town I'm not at all familiar with. The houses here are boxy, brick affairs with narrow windows fitted with air conditioning units. It's obvious they were ugly even when they were built, and that must have been decades ago, judging by the condition they're in. There's a reason I've never been to this side of town. People on my side of town like to pretend this side doesn't exist.

"Just make it quick," Royal says, shutting off the engine of his brand-new Range Rover.

"You know, you wouldn't have to shuttle me around if you'd convince Daddy to let me drive."

"When you get a license, you can drive," Royal says with a smug smile.

"Which will never happen if you don't let me practice."

"You think I'm letting you practice on my new baby?" he asks with mock shock.

"I wouldn't run it into any parked cars," I shoot back. "So I'm already a better driver than you."

"No license, no driving," he says. "Go see your dead girl. I've got shit to do."

I roll my eyes at Dixie, and she hops out and leads me across a small stretch of dead grass to a creaky iron gate. We enter the cemetery, which stretches back quite a way. The headstones are mostly small, with faded plastic flowers on many of them. An old white church sits beside it, the paint peeling along the bottom boards and stained with lichen and dust.

"This is depressing," I mutter as we make our way back along a path worn through the grass. Three figures approach on the path, two men and a petite woman, backlit by the setting sun. We're probably the last people to visit today, as I don't see anyone else.

"It's a cemetery," Dixie says. "I think the point is to be depressing."

A chill works its way through me, and I clutch the bouquet we bought on the way here to my chest. This could have been the end result last year. It almost was. A few more minutes in that pool, and it would have ended differently. If her mom had gotten home five minutes later, if she'd hit two more red lights, if she'd fed the dog first when she walked in the house, if she'd put away the groceries before looking for her daughter. I try to imagine how I'd feel if I had to visit that girl's grave, and another shudder wracks my body, making me clutch the flowers even tighter.

The three figures step into the shadow of the church, revealing more than their silhouettes, and I lurch to a halt. One of them is Devlin Darling.

My heart stutters in my chest, and the world sways under me. He wasn't at school today, so I haven't seen him since the not-accident yesterday morning.

Beside him, a petite blonde girl clings to the arm of a tall, gorgeous guy with piercing blue eyes and tousled blond hair. The girl's eyes are red and puffy, as if she's been crying. The guy on her arm looks somber, as does Devlin. But when Devlin's eyes sweep over us, they harden to flint.

"Dixie Powell?" says the blond guy with the somber face. His expression breaks into a big, friendly grin, the corners of his eyes crinkling and the sober surroundings apparently forgotten. He pulls his arm from the petite blonde and wraps Dixie in a big hug.

She looks like she's about to faint, and I swear she swells to twice her usual size with the pride of being recognized by the hottie.

"I told Linds that Willow Heights must have poached you," he says, pulling back and shooting Devlin a mock glare. "Bastards."

"What are you doing here?" Devlin grinds out, glaring at Dixie as if he can't bear to look at me. A handful of tiny white petals dot one shoulder of his navy jacket, and his hair is tousled by the wind. I tear my eyes away from him, looking at the couple beside him. I don't recognize them from Willow Heights.

"Today's the anniversary of her death, right?" Dixie says, shrinking back to her usual size beside me.

Anger flares inside me, but I keep my mouth shut and try to ignore Devlin as thoroughly as he's ignoring me.

"You didn't even know her," Devlin says, yanking the flowers out of my arms. "Neither of you. Go home."

By now, Dixie's shrunken even smaller, down to the sniveling dog I met on my first day. "Do you own this cemetery?" I ask, swiping for the flowers.

Devlin holds them out of my reach. "Tell me her name," he says, his eyes boring into mine.

"I don't know her name," I say flatly. "I'm here to support my friend. That's it. Now, if you don't own this cemetery, I suggest you get out of our way, because this has nothing to do with you."

Devlin stares at me incredulously. "Nothing to do with me?" he asks. "She died at my fucking house, Crystal. And people like you want to make a spectacle of it by parading by, shedding your fake tears and pretending to give a fuck when you can't even bother to learn her name. It's Destiny. And she's not a sideshow."

He drops the flowers on the ground and steps on them as he shoves past us and walks away.

The blonde girl is crying again, clinging to the friendly boy's arm. He gives us an apologetic shrug and picks up the flowers, handing them back. They're broken and dirty, but I take them just the same. Dixie seems frozen in place, all the color drained from her face.

"Sorry," the blond guy mutters, and he puts an arm around his girl and leads her away, following Devlin.

"You okay?" I ask, turning to Dixie.

She nods, swallowing hard. "Thanks. I can't believe you did that for me. You're a good friend, Crystal."

"Rules of friendship," I say with a shrug.

"First rule," she says with a weak smile. "Have each other's backs."

"You wanna just leave?" I ask, taking her arm. I knew this was a bad idea, though I had expected family to be there, not Devlin Darling.

Unless he is family. Shit.

I swallow the fist lodged in my throat and glance over my shoulder. The only car left in the lot is Royal's.

"No," Dixie says. "We brought her flowers. It's not like we're just here to gawk."

That's exactly what it's like. Devlin's words cut to the bone—because they're true. Dixie didn't go to Willow Heights last year, so she didn't know the girl any better than I did. We came simply for the sensational gossip.

Did you hear…

Could it really be true?

Did a girl really die at a Darling party?

Turns out, it's really fucking true. Now that I know it's real, that a real person, a person our age, is under the ground in one of these plots, the last thing I want to do is go stand over her bones.

"Come on," Dixie says, grabbing the tattered flowers from my arms and marching toward the back of the cemetery, her red hair flying. My standing up for her seems to have lit a fire under her ass, and she can't wait to defy Devlin, too. I grudgingly admire her for it, even if I don't really want to follow her. She's never been here, but it doesn't take a genius to find Destiny's grave.

It's piled with so many white flowers that it looks like a funeral shroud covers the grass in front of her headstone. I swallow hard and take a step in that direction, my knees threatening to buckle. All I can think about is the girl under there, a girl who wanted to jump into a pool, not to die but to be brave. To get applause, to get slaps on the back and screams of admiration. She didn't sink to the bottom and inhale chlorine. Her mother didn't find her floating, facedown, with her hair fanned out around her head.

Who called her parents? Who told them? Who pulled her out of the water? Who realized she wasn't swimming, that she hadn't come up?

I sink to my knees beside the bed of white flowers covering her like a down comforter. I imagine lying under there, under six feet of earth and the weight of a blanket of grief, how heavy it would be. How it would hold you down and trap you, so you could never rise again.

"I don't think you should be friends with me," I choke out, staring at the white petals around my knees.

"What?" Dixie asks. "Are you okay, Crystal? What's wrong?"

"Devlin's going to make my life hell," I say. "You saw how much he hates me. I can't involve you in that."

"So far as I can tell, he hates everyone," Dixie says. "And besides, I was already the Darling Dog. He can't do much worse than that."

"Remember when I asked you to be my friend?" I say. "I told you I'd done all the head cheerleader stuff, that I wasn't a very good person."

"Yeah…"

172

"I'm not good," I say, my voice barely above a whisper. "I'm not a good person."

"But you said you were starting over," Dixie says. "I mean, yeah, your brothers have done some pretty bad stuff, but you haven't done anything bad since you got here. I think people should get a second chance even if they did something bad before."

"What if what they did was unforgiveable?" I ask the ground in front of me, where a dead girl lies buried. "I was worse than Devlin. I didn't just call someone a dog. I... I almost did this to her."

"What?" Dixie asks, lowering herself to the ground beside me.

"The worst part is, I don't even know why," I whisper. "I didn't even know the girl."

"Who was she?" Dixie asked. "Someone in New York?"

"Yeah, she went our school. She was just... She was one of those girls who tries so hard it's too hard, you know? Like, she'd insert herself into conversations she overheard that didn't involve her. She was so desperate about wanting to be part of everything. And for some reason, my friend just got it in her head that she hated this girl. She couldn't stand her."

"And you went along with it because your best friend hated her."

"Yes," I admit, shame burning in my cheeks. "I didn't at first. I told her to leave the girl alone, but she'd comment on her posts online and mock her at school when she was being desperate. And the girl, she didn't do anything. She wouldn't stand up for herself. It was infuriating. You just wanted to shake her and tell her to have some self-respect."

"Like me," Dixie says softly.

"No," I say quickly. "Not like you."

But maybe she's right. Maybe that's part of what drew me to Dixie. I never knew that girl, never knew what was going on in her head or why she was that way, and maybe in some subconscious way, I wanted to understand.

"Veronica was my co-captain on the cheer squad, and a year older than me," I say. "Even when I felt like things were good, I always felt like I was walking on thin ice. I was only a sophomore, and I knew I'd gotten the co-captain spot partly because she had put in a good word for me. She knew how hard I worked, how many nights I stayed up practicing routines until four in the morning."

"Then it sounds like you deserved it," Dixie says, her freckled face so earnest I want to hug her. "You earned it."

"Yeah," I say softly. "But it wasn't just that. It's all about who you know, who you impress, who's on your side. I was popular, Dixie, but I was miserable. I was in therapy and taking medication, but I couldn't stop feeling like the ground was going to drop out from under me at any moment. Like if I made wrong move, everything I'd built for myself would come crashing down."

"Because of your friend?"

I laugh softly and tell her something I've never told anyone. "You know that lipstick I always wear? I called it my signature color."

"It looks good on you," Dixie says.

"The funny thing is, I don't even like it that much," I say. "I mean, it's fine, but it's no better than any other color. But it wore it one day in eighth grade, and Veronica said she liked it. After that, I felt like if I wore any other color, she might tell me it wasn't flattering, or that I looked bad. So I wore that lipstick every single day for the next two years. And the thing is, she probably wouldn't have said anything. It wasn't even her. It was me. It was like this superstition, like when a guy wears the same undershirt for every game because he's convinced if he wears something else, his team will lose. I was so miserably scared every second of every day even though I had what every girl wants."

"Why didn't you just quit?" Dixie asks, as if it's that simple. Maybe it is.

"I guess I did," I say. "But not then. Not until that girl. Veronica would pick on her, and I'd just stand there feeling sick. And I remember thinking, she's so pathetic. Why doesn't she leave Veronica alone? But she kept coming back, like a dog that wants to be kicked just so it can have some attention. I kept telling myself, why should I stand up for her if she won't stand up for herself?

"I remember the first day I said something to her, and it was just some little cutting comment, but I felt like dirt afterwards. It didn't make me feel good or powerful. It made me feel even smaller. And the sick thing is, that didn't stop me. It was like, some part of me liked that. I started getting meaner because I just wanted her to finally snap and push back against all of it. But she never did."

"She died?" Dixie asks, her eyes widening.

"No," I say. "She tried, though. That's when everything changed. The school got involved, saw all the horrible things we'd said to her online. Mostly it was Veronica, but I did it, too. And not just when we were together, and she'd tell me to. It was like I saw weakness, and I hated it. I just wanted to stamp it out. And the sad part is, there was no reason for any of it. She didn't steal anyone's boyfriend or get someone kicked off the squad. That's the part that really fucks with my head. There was no reason."

"Maybe not a good one," Dixie says. "Probably she just reminded you of yourself. How bad you wanted to impress your friend, and how you felt like you couldn't stand up to her. So you wanted someone else to."

I nod, waiting for the ache in my throat to dissolve. "I don't want to take you down with me," I say. "If Devlin wants revenge, and he saw us together today…"

"You haven't done anything to him," she points out. "Your brother wrecked his car. Not you. There's no reason for him to hate you."

"Does he need a reason?" I asked. "Did he have a reason for making you the Darling Dog?"

Dixie's cheeks redden in the fading daylight. "I mean, some other people were picking on me first. And then he came along and claimed me for him and his brothers. No one else dares to say a word to me now. I'm not saying what you did wasn't brave and good and everything, but…" She shakes her head.

"You liked him picking on you?"

She shrugs, her face going even redder. "It's not that," she says quickly. "But like… I know what I look like, Crystal." She gives me a hard look.

"You're sexy," I say. "You have curves. Guys like that."

"I'm fat," she says. "And, like, I know I'm supposed to care, but I don't even really want to change that. I'm okay with it."

"Which is fine."

"Yeah, but guys like the Darlings? They want girls who are curvy like you."

"He labeled me a dog, too," I point out. "I don't think it matters what you look like. They just pick people at random to terrorize everyone else into falling in line."

Dixie shrugs. "Still. They'd never give a girl like me the time of day. When I was the Darling Dog, though…"

I rub my forehead. "Dixie. That's fucked up. You don't have to choose between being treated like a dog and being invisible."

"Maybe not," she says. "But if I want to be visible to guys like them?" She closes her eyes and groans. "And I do. I'm sorry, I know it's as pathetic as that girl wanting your friend to pay attention to her, but oh my god, Crystal. They're the *Darlings.*"

"Well, I think what he's doing is sick. And I'm going to stop them. No more Darling Dogs."

Dixie stares at me like I'm crazy. "You can't do that."

"Maybe not," I say, standing and holding out a hand. "But I'm going to try."

"How?" Dixie asks, letting me pull her to her feet before wiping her hands on her skirt.

"I don't know," I say. "But I've been there. If anyone understands a bully, it's me."

fifteen

There's only one way to win with bullies if you don't want to join them. My brothers have erased any possibility of joining them, and I probably couldn't have changed their ways anyway. I made the mistake of joining a bully before. Which leaves only one option with the Darlings. Beat them.

The only question is, how?

The next day, the ax falls. The entire school is buzzing with news from the moment we walk in. People shoot us dirty looks, and as we walk down the hall, a chorus of deep, furious woofs follows us. I walk forward on trembling legs, keeping my eyes straight ahead. My brothers don't know this is for me alone. They haven't witnessed it before.

When we arrive at my locker, Royal touches my elbow. "You okay?"

"Fine," I say, twisting the combination lock.

Duke grins and blows kisses to the masses, seemingly oblivious to the hatred that accompanies the barking. For him, attention is attention. He's eating it up.

"Once they see us play, they'll be singing a different tune," Baron says, leaning against the locker next to mine.

"They'll be groveling on the floor for a chance to suck our dicks," Duke says. "And I'll remind them exactly how much they have to make up for."

Royal walks me to class, where even Colt doesn't want to sit with me. I figure out the hate, though. Preston is suspended from the next game, which is Homecoming. Devlin is suspended from the team indefinitely. I know it's perfect, just what my brothers wanted. But I can't help but think of the other side of it. Just as Dixie reminded me that I deserved my spot on the cheer squad at my last school, I know that Devlin's position isn't one he takes for granted. I hear him out there throwing the ball almost every night. He's worked for that position for who knows how long. And here come my brothers, ready to steal it out from under him. He didn't do anything to deserve that.

I wonder what he'll have left by the time the Dolces are done with him. He's lost his beautiful car. He's lost his place on the team. According to Dixie he doesn't date, but from the number of days that both Dolly and Preston leave class together, I'm pretty sure he doesn't even have his biggest fan anymore.

That night, when I can't sleep, I stand on my balcony listening to the silence in the Darlings' backyard. A single light is on upstairs, and I stare at the gentle glow inside the rectangle, willing Devlin to appear. But the house remains quiet. He threatened to break me, but I'm afraid my brothers have broken him first. He has given up his midnight practice, and at school, he avoids me entirely.

A thought worms its way into my mind, refusing to leave. What if I'm not the only bully in my family? A cool wind rustles the magnolia in the backyard, and I pull the belt of my robe tight around me, but I can't seem to get warm. I can't shake the lingering thought, even when I go back inside and lock the door, close the curtains, and crawl into bed, pulling my pillows over my head. What my brothers are doing, that's not the same as what I did. They saw something they wanted, and they went for it. That's what people are supposed to do.

People aren't supposed to cut down another person for no reason. That's what I did. It's totally different than what my brothers are doing. They're ambitious, determined, and persevering. I was small and mean and weak. That's the difference. My brothers are strong, a force to be reckoned with. I'm weak. I saw that in another person, and I wanted to destroy it. They don't care who the Darlings are or what they want. If the Darlings didn't exist, they'd still want the same thing.

I roll over, pressing the pillow down over my ears, as if I can block out the silence of Devlin not practicing. This is silly. My brothers aren't bad. They just don't take no for an answer. They know what they want, and they take it. They just don't care who they have to step on to get it.

*

Friday rolls around at last, and with some trepidation, I agree to join my brothers at the homecoming game. We all pile into the Range Rover and go to pick up Dixie. She lives in a regular subdivision in a new house that could be found in the suburbs of any city anywhere. She rushes out and flings open the door, her words cutting off when she sees all of my brothers in the car with me. Her cheeks turn pink, and her eyes go wide with fear, as if she's afraid we're playing a horrible trick on her and we're going to speed off laughing.

"Hop that fat ass up here on my lap," Duke says, patting his thigh and grinning at her.

"Don't call her that," I say, throwing an elbow into his side.

"Hey, it's not an insult," he says, taking Dixie's hand and helping her onto his lap. "If she wasn't your friend, I'd have my dick buried ten inches deep in this ass."

"Cut it out," King snaps from the front seat.

"Thank you," I say. "I don't think my friend needs to hear about your perversions, especially not when she's sitting in your lap."

"Don't knock it 'til you try it," Duke says, squeezing Dixie's hips. "Am I right?"

She lets out a squeal of laughter, blushing even harder than she usually does around my brothers.

When we get to the game, the parking lot is packed. You'd think it was a Patriot's game the way people have decked out their cars in black and gold. Windows are painted with "Go Knights," along with various jersey numbers.

As we climb out of the car, a group of fans goes tearing through the parking lot carrying a huge black flag with a gold knight insignia on it. They're all wearing Knights jerseys and full face paint.

I catch my brothers glancing at each other. King grins, and I can feel the excitement radiating off them as we head for the gates. Not just excitement at watching a football game, but excitement at this new and very welcome change from our old school. Sure, people went to those games. Parents of players, other students, and a few alumni. This is so much bigger than that.

After the uneasy week at school, it's nice to see my brothers bursting with positive energy again. One look in Royal's dark eyes, and I know I was being too hard on them the other night. Royal might be as fucked up as the rest of us, but he's good and strong and protective, and he'd do anything for me.

I give him a quick hug before falling back to walk next to Dixie.

"It looks like the entire town is here," I comment, searching the crowd automatically, not realizing I'm looking for Devlin until the little surge of hope inside me dies when I don't find him.

"Yeah," she says. "We're playing Faulkner High."

"Ah," I say, remembering that Daddy mentioned them. "Our public school rival."

"We only play them once every season," Dixie says. "And maybe once in the playoffs. Whoever wins has bragging rights for the entire year. I'm sure the Darlings have been over there pranking their school all week. They barely even remembered we exist this week."

"You say that like it's a bad thing," I say. "Besides, I think my brothers have kept them busy."

She shrugs and looks up at the stands. "Faulkner won last year. So, this is our big chance to get even. The whole town waits for this game every season."

I try to comprehend a game that big in New York. Besides the Superbowl, there's nothing that could get the whole city excited over a football game. And the apocalypse itself couldn't shut down stores.

"Maybe you'll see your graveyard hottie," I say, nudging her elbow with mine.

"Who?" she asks, her eyes widening.

I roll my eyes. "Don't pretend you don't know."

"That's just a guy I went to elementary with," she says, her cheeks going pink. "I don't even know him anymore."

"He sure seemed to know you," I tease.

"He was with his girlfriend," she points out. "Who, I might add, is another one of the Darling cousins."

"And she goes to Faulkner High?" I ask, covering my heart and pretending to be scandalized.

"I think it has more to do with her boyfriend than anything," she says. "They definitely live in the right part of town."

"Well, I guess you shouldn't go after him," I say. "Or the Darling's will put a hit out on you."

Speaking of, I glance around, making sure all my brothers are within my line of sight. I keep waiting for the retribution. I know better than to think Devlin's had enough. If he's anything like my brothers, there will never be enough now. He's got a grudge, and he won't stop until he's carried through with a punishment warranted by the crime.

"Let's get popcorn," Daddy says. He lowers his voice and winks at me. "Gotta support the local economy, after all. It's good to let people know you care."

I'm not sure how much he actually cares and how much he just wants to be seen, but I don't say it. I know appearances are everything for a family like ours. If this is a community event, you can be damn sure Daddy will be there, the star of his family show, surrounded by his beautiful offspring.

I suddenly feel disloyal for my thoughts. Daddy loves football. Maybe he really is excited about the game, about scoping out the competition just like my brothers are. If anyone's more excited about them getting on the team than they are, it's him. He may want to look like the star of the Dolce clan, but he wants us to be the stars of everything else.

Whatever matters most to our school, we should be at the very center of that.

"Let's go get seats," Royal says, taking my elbow and steering me toward the stands. I glance back over my shoulder, but King falls in on my other side, his presence reassuring me. The Darlings aren't going to do anything here, in front of the whole town. I'm reminded of that when I see the cop who arrested them chatting with some locals. Devlin's probably not even here. He's at home, most likely cooking up some horrible revenge scheme with Preston right now.

The bleachers are packed with people of all ages, from moms with babies to great-grandparents. Half of them are talking while the other half cheer even though the players aren't on the field. The cheerleaders start a chant and everyone in the stands starts yelling along with them. I spot Lacey, my guide from the first day, in the squad. No surprise there. Anyone deigned worthy of being a Darling Doll, of sitting with the cousins at lunch if there's enough space at their table by the time she arrives, must be popular.

King nudges me. "Check out the cheerleaders while we're here."

"Not really into girls, but thanks."

He gives me an annoyed glance. "You need to know what you're up against."

"I don't think I'm really into the whole cheering thing anymore."

"Tell that to Dad," he says, guiding me along a row of metal bleachers to a space just big enough for us to ask a couple if they can scoot down to make room for the seven of us. The night is cool, and the woman has a black fleece blanket draped across her knees with the Willow Heights crest on it. These people take their football really fucking serious.

Half the stands are filled with people shaking black and gold pompoms. I look around in awe, not sure if I'm more intimidated or impressed by the sight. If I got on the cheer squad, I'd be under scrutiny from the entire town. Literally. Across the way, the Faulkner High stands are just as crazy. One look at the crowd, and I already know Faulkner's colors are navy and white.

On the field on their side, a redheaded cheerleader is yelling at her squad. Her back is to her crowd, but I can tell from all the way across the field that she's pissed. Glad she's not the team captain I'll have to impress. Not that I'm going out for cheer. I'll get my therapist to recommend against it if Dad can't be reasoned with.

"Cheer tryouts were last year," Dixie says. Her cheeks redden, and she ducks her head. For a second, I think she's still nervous around my brothers, but then I realize that's not it.

"You tried out?" I ask.

"It's stupid," she mumbles. "Like you ever see a cheerleader who looks like me up there."

"That's bullshit," I burst out. "There are all kinds of cheerleaders."

"Really?" Dixie asks, nodding at the girls. I look them over, noting how entirely homogenous the Willow Heights side is. There's one biracial girl, but otherwise, the most diversity apparent on the squad is a petite girl with a bob. Otherwise, every single girl is white, slender, and with a long pony swinging behind her. The two boys on the squad look like body builders-in-training.

"What bullshit," I mutter. "You should get to be on the squad if you're good."

"Are you?" Dixie asks. "I mean, you were captain of your last squad."

"Yeah," I say with a shrug. "I'm good."

"She's really fucking good," Royal says, putting an arm around me and squeezing.

It's true. I was good. I worked for it, but that just made me want it all the more. I'd be lying if I said there isn't a part of me aching to be down there, that my fingers aren't twitching to hold a pompon, that I'm not watching every step of their choreography.

But after it all went down last year, I didn't want to paste a smile on my face and cheer. I didn't want to be on top of the pyramid, or even the social ladder. I wanted to disappear. It was spring, so there was less for us to do than during football season. I stayed on the squad because I had a note from my psychiatrist, but I knew I wouldn't cheer again in the fall.

Now, though... This is a new school. A big part of me thinks it would be a mistake to go after a spot on the squad, just like my brothers are doing for football. If I take a spot, I take someone's place. Someone who tried out and earned that spot, someone who might have stayed up all night practicing routines just like I did.

On the other hand, I'm better than at least half the girls out there. And if they're really such bitches they'd cut Dixie because she's a little bigger than they are, I want to do something about it.

"How good are you?" I ask, turning to Dixie.

"What?"

"How good are you? Maybe we can change their minds."

"What are you talking about?" she asks, her eyes widening. "You can't just… I mean, I'm pretty good, I guess. I haven't practiced in months, though. I stopped after I didn't make it."

"Then start again," I say. "I will, too. We'll show these bitches what we can do."

sixteen

There's something about high school football that no other sport can touch. It's in the lights, the chill in the evening air, the fans in the bleachers. It's in the green grass and the white lines, the smell of popcorn and the crackle of the loudspeaker. To be a part of that, to stand on the sidelines and cheer, was magic. But the field has more than magic. It has power. It's power leaches up through cleats and carries through the halls at school. Tonight, my brothers make a power grab.

"What are you doing?" Dixie asks, peering over my shoulder.

"Nothing," I say, shoving my phone into my pocket without posting the blog. I glance over to make sure my brothers are engaged in conversation and won't ask the same thing.

"You're always writing on your phone," Dixie says. When I don't answer, she pushes her elbow against mine. "Spill. You have to tell me. No secrets. Rules of friendship, remember?"

"It's nothing important," I say, lowering my voice to near a whisper. "I just have a blog."

"Really?" she asks, leaning in like I'm sharing juicy gossip. "Do you have a lot of followers?"

"Um, no," I say. "It's private. No one can read it but me. It's just... A way to express myself. Like a diary that my brothers can't find and look through."

"So, they don't know?" she whispers, glancing past me to them.

"No," I say. "And I plan to keep it that way, so shut up about it, okay?"

She mines zippering her lips, a smile shining in her eyes that makes my heart squeeze for her. It's like she's never had a real friend before, never shared anyone's secret. I want to hug her and shake her at the same time. She's so impossibly transparent.

Dad and the twins appear a minute later, loaded down with popcorn, soda, and candy. Apparently Daddy was serious about supporting the local economy. It looks like he bought out the entire concession stand. As soon as he sits down, he starts scoping the stands. A flare of irritation goes through me when I realize what he's doing. He's looking for someone important, making sure they see him. Just like last week, when he stood me up for our father-daughter time because some city planner wanted to chat over drinks.

Sure enough, a minute later he hands me his soda and says, "I'm just going to say hello to someone. I'll be right back."

"I thought we were showing up as a family," I say. I've barely seen him since we moved here. That's no different from life back home, but he promised things would be different here. That he'd have more time for us.

"We are," Daddy says. "It'll just be a minute. This is important."

And we're not?

I want to ask, but I pinch my lips together and nod.

"He'll be back," Dixie says, patting my knee and giving me a sympathetic smile. It nearly makes me crack. I may not be strong, but I don't want anyone's pity. It makes me vulnerable, and I want no part of that. Not in public.

Daddy's already halfway down the aisle, obviously not needing my agreement for him to ditch us. Royal scowls after him, then scoots over and slides an arm around my shoulders. "What do you think?"

"That he's going to make us sit with the headmaster?" I offer, trying to smile.

He frowns even more deeply and squeezes me against him. "I'm sorry."

"You weren't talking about him, though, were you?"

"No."

"It's… Intense," I admit as the band comes on, and everyone in the stands sings along with the fight song. It's more like a college game than a high school game. Only the small stadium with the banks of lights at the ends, the scruffy real grass on the field, and the family atmosphere speak of a high school game.

The cheerleaders cede the field to a row of six majorettes. I spot Dolly among them, not a stitch of pink in sight. She looks one hundred percent bombshell in the fitted black leotard with gold sparkles glinting like stars from the stretchy fabric. Her curves put mine to shame. While I've never been unhappy about my "perfect Cs" as Veronica called them, Dolly must wear an F-cup. Her hips are wide and round, too, but she's not built like a Kardashian. Her belly curves out a bit, too, and her thighs aren't leaving a gap anytime soon. She's just a big girl all over—tall, curvy, and thick.

"I think I just spotted my first wife," Duke jokes, obviously looking at the same person I am. It's hard not to look at her. All the majorettes are wearing the same thing, but no one is wearing it quite like Dolly. Her blonde hair is done up in a tall updo, and she's wearing potent red lipstick and fake lashes so black and long that they don't even attempt to look real. They have gold glitter in them that catches the light when she moves.

Royal nudges me, and I follow his nod to see Daddy waving for us to join him. He's standing beside a tall, thin man with receding salt-and-pepper hair and a sharp nose. Beside him is a blonde of indeterminate age who could just as easily be his daughter as his wife.

Great. Time to smile and be a good Dolce daughter.

"Sorry," I mutter to Dixie. "You don't have to come with us."

She looks between Daddy and us. "Crap on a cracker," she says, her eyes widening. "That's my aunt."

"The one who just married the mayor?"

"The one who called me unkempt," Dixie confirms.

"I'll just go say hi," I say, anxiety flaring inside me at the feeling of being pulled in two directions like I was with Veronica. I want to be a good friend, but I also want to be a good daughter. I want my father to be happy, but I don't want to violate the rules of friendship—and not just the dorky list Dixie made—by telling him something they wouldn't want an adult to know.

"It's okay," Dixie says. "We'll all be happier if we pretend we don't see each other. I usually sit over there with the other freshmen, anyway. Come sit with us when you get done."

Dixie goes off to mingle with some people who are apparently her friends even though she never sits with them at lunch. Maybe it's something that happens at football games here. It brings everyone together, the whole town cheering. At a game, everyone wearing black and gold is a friend. At a school this small, it's inevitable that people will fall into the groups where they fit best. Even the outcasts usually get shuffled together. And Dixie's too chipper to be an outcast. I'm happy for her if she's making other friends, even if it does awaken my insecurity. Rules of Friendship aside, Dixie's not the Darling Dog anymore. I am. If she wants to call me toxic and stay away from me, that's fair. She's more than fulfilled any obligation to me.

A tightness builds inside me as we gather our things. I imagine mingling with the crowd, saying hi to random people from school, not worrying about anything but the outcome of the game. But I already know I can't escape who I am. Who we are. Where my father goes, we all go. When Daddy says jump, we jump. When he says we're going to be the primo family in this town, we make it happen for him.

As we arrive beside him, Daddy gives the twins a stern look, a silent warning that they'd better behave. My brothers aren't exactly model citizens.

Daddy introduces his new friends as Mayor and Mrs. Beckett.

SELENA

"It's wonderful to see some fresh faces at Willow Heights." Mayor Beckett grips my hand a little too long, examining my chest a little too long. Ew. I tug my hand away, making sure my face doesn't betray my disgust. I've dealt with plenty of Daddy's slimy business associates in my life. I'm supposed to be the little angel, too innocent to even notice when they leer at my body and "accidentally" brush my ass when I walk by. At least they're all smart enough not to make a real move. If Daddy didn't have them killed for that, my brothers would make it happen.

"You and the mayor sit in the crowd for football games," I say to Mrs. Beckett as we take our seats. "Let's just say that never happened at our private school in New York."

I expect at least a chuckle, but Mrs. Beckett only raises her brows and picks an invisible speck of lint from her black pantsuit. "My husband thinks it's important to look like one of the people."

"And he's absolutely right," Daddy says. "You have to know what's going on in your town if you want people to trust you enough to come to you with important issues."

He's too busy kissing the mayor's ass to notice he just pissed off his wife, who obviously wants to be sitting in the one box up by the announcer. Or more likely, to be at home having a cocktail and watching the game on TV.

"Do you guys come to all the games?" I ask Mrs. Beckett. "Or just the one that's your entire town?"

"Most of them," she says, casting a withering look at her husband, who's busy chatting with Daddy about new businesses coming to town and how it helps the economy.

"Do you always sit on our side?" I ask, giving her my best conspiratorial smile. "Or do you have to sit with Faulkner High fans every other year?"

"Well, we're here as mayor, but his daughter also cheers."

"Oh, yeah?" I ask, perking up. This is definitely pertinent information if I'm going to woo the cheer squad into letting me—and her step-niece—join partway through the season. I wonder why Dixie never mentioned it. "Which one is she?"

"Dolly Beckett," the mayor's wife says.

"Oh," I say, quickly masking my surprise. "I should have known. She looks just like you."

Majorettes don't cheer. Her mother should know that.

Mrs. Beckett sniffs. "She's my stepdaughter."

"Oh, right! I'm sorry." I'm too flustered to say more. Apparently, I'm not good at schmoozing in Arkansas, either.

"Of course she is," King says, swooping in to save me. "I would have thought she was your sister."

Thank fuck for my brothers. I shove a Twizzler into my mouth before I can put my foot in there again. I'm happy to let King flirt and charm Mrs. Beckett while I watch the cheerleaders do a quick routine and then move to the sidelines. The bleachers begin to shake as everyone in the stands pounds their feet in unison, faster and faster, drumming excitement into the air as the announcer comes on. His voice booms out over the field.

"Let's make some noise for the Faulkner High Wampus Cats!"

The other side goes crazy, throwing popcorn into the air, stomping the bleachers, and screaming.

"What the fuck is a wampus cat?" Duke asks.

"It's a six-legged wildcat," Baron says. "Haven't you ever read Harry Potter?"

"No," Duke shoots back. "Haven't you ever gotten laid?"

"Tonight's matchup is one of legend," the announcer goes on. "Let's welcome our hometown rivals, Devlin Darling and the Knights!"

I stiffen in my seat, shock knifing through me. Surely they didn't let him back on the team already. There's video of him assaulting my brother while he's clearly passed out on the ground.

"I've just been informed that the Knights' star players, Devlin and Preston Darling, won't be playing tonight's game," the announcer says after a short pause. "That'll put a crimp in their style, but I'd say it's still going to be one heck of a matchup. Let's show Willow Heights our support!"

Our side of the stands cheers and shakes their pretty pompoms, but we're not as loud or wild as the public school fans. Their side looks like they might riot if they lose. Or maybe it's because they just announced their school like a regular team, and they announced ours like a band fronted by a famous rock star.

From the first play, the game doesn't look promising. Faulkner wins the coin toss, and their quarterback makes a series of smart plays, getting them within field goal range before they have to turn it over. Our quarterback, the backup for Devlin, proceeds to make some seriously questionable passes, which leads to a third and long and then an interception.

I look over at King, and despite Willow Heights' poor performance, he's grinning broadly. Of course he is. Devlin might rule the school, but while he's suspended, our school could definitely use a smart quarterback our brother.

Faulkner scores another field goal, and then we turn it over. It looks bad until Colt catches an interception and runs all the way in for a touchdown. If I expected Colt to be slow and lazy on the field like he is in class, I'm in for a disappointment. He's fast—really fast. Again I get that sense that his school persona is all an act, that he's more than he shows the world.

We're behind by two touchdowns at halftime, and I get up to stretch my legs—and to avoid making small talk with the sleazy mayor and his grumpy wife. I'm starting to get nervous that they're going to blame us for the game's outcome. After all, my brothers got the Darlings suspended.

Everyone is milling around, chatting in excited voices about Colt's touchdown or just hanging out. The buzz of the crowd, and the lights, and the cool October night wash over me, sending a little chill of familiarity through me even as I stand alone in the concession line.

In front of me stands Dolly Beckett. Great. Now I get to stare at her ass and wonder what's going on with her and Devlin. Does she know he worried about his game enough to be up at midnight, throwing passes? Or that for the last week, since we wrecked his car and got him thrown off the team, he no longer practices? Would she care?

After all, she likes to slip out of class and rendezvous with Preston nearly every day. And why do I care whether she's thinking about Devlin or Preston tonight?

I shove the thought away. I don't care.

"I think he did it on purpose," Dolly says to her friend, another majorette. "I mean, it's like he wants to get hurt sometimes."

"He wouldn't get suspended on purpose," her friend says. "We need him. The team is falling apart without him."

Dolly sighs. "I'm just saying. You've seen the way he throws himself around out there. It's like he has no regard for personal safety."

I perk up. This is information my brothers will want. So, Devlin's reckless for a quarterback. Someone like Royal would never make the mistakes his second-string QB is making, and he's not careless.

"Do you think he noticed me before the game?" Dolly asks.

I roll my eyes, thinking there's no way that any straight man in attendance could have failed to notice her. But then someone behind me repeats her words in a high, mocking voice, and I immediately feel guilty for my own unkind thoughts. Dolly's face flushes, but she ignores the girl and keeps looking at her friend, who offers her a pitying smile.

I turn to see Lacey and a couple girls from the cheer squad flipping their ponytails and laughing. They look right through me and keep talking. "They know not to address royalty directly. They're just a bunch of wanna-be cheerleaders."

An absurd urge to defend Dolly rises in me, and even though I know better than to go up against the hierarchy around here, I can't help myself. After all, she's not a Doll anymore, which means she's not as untouchable as she once was.

"Shouldn't you be back on the field boring the fans to sleep with more of your unoriginal cheers?" I ask lightly.

Lacey's mouth falls open in a huff of disbelief.

"Stay out of this," says another cheerleader I recognize as Carmen from my Spanish class. "This is none of your business, little city bitch."

I smirk at her and raise an eyebrow. "Is that the best you can do?" I ask. "Even your insults are unoriginal. Oh, and just so you know, I'm a big city bitch."

Lacey hooks her arm through Carmen's. "Don't pay attention to her," she says. "She's just mad because she'll never be a Darling Doll. She's just Devlin's little lap dog."

"And yet, you got on your knees and ate dogfood when he ordered you to," I say. "So remind me again what's the difference between a Darling Dog and a Doll?"

"She can't be serious," Lacey says.

I shrug and slide my hand along my sleek pony. "I just know I wasn't the one eating dogfood that day." I turn to face forward again, noticing that Dolly and her friend are whispering, their heads bent together. If she wants to run and tell Preston, fine. Whatever. I'm not keeping my mouth shut and being anyone's obedient pet, no matter what they call me.

By now I know that being a Darling Dog isn't as bad as it sounds. Sure, I've been labeled aa loser, but besides the one humiliating incident and the outburst after we got the Darlings in trouble, it's pretty mild. They didn't even condone the dogfood incident, so I can't count that as a consequence of being labeled. I can handle a lot worse a few snickers and snide comments when I walk by. I deserve a lot worse.

When I get back to our seats, Baron pats the spot beside him. "Dad's talked the mayor into going to see the coach with us," he says. "We're all going to go talk him, show him what we can bring to the table."

"Tonight?" I ask, once again surprised and impressed with how skillfully Daddy manipulates.

"Yeah," Duke says with a broad smile. "Right after the game. If they keep getting creamed the entire game, it shouldn't be hard to make a case for ourselves."

"Congratulations," I say, throwing an arm around each twin. My brothers are good. If they get a tryout, they're as good as on the team. And with the mayor on our side, how can the coach say no?

I tell my brothers what I overheard Dolly saying about Devlin being too reckless, but a funny little flicker goes through me when they start discussing it. I don't owe Devlin or Dolly any loyalty, but for some reason, it feels like a betrayal. What's the use in spying if you're not going to use the information, though?

seventeen

Tonight, my brothers finish what they started. Tonight, they topple the kings. Tonight is theirs for the taking. Whatever the consequences, we'll face them as they come. But tonight, we triumph.

After the game, we start down to the field. I tell my family I'll meet them outside the locker room, and I run to the restroom. They'll be with the coach for a while, so I have plenty of time. A line has formed out of the restroom, so I step outside and lean against the wall under a light and finish my blog post before texting Dixie. The Knights lost, so everyone from Willow Heights is in a foul mood, but I can't help but smile inside. It would have been a tougher sell to get my brothers on the team after a win against our biggest rival.

After a loss, the coach will be looking at all the things the team did wrong—and all the things my brothers can do better.

I text Dixie for a few minutes before a shadow falls over me. I jerk upright just in time to see Devlin Darling towering over me. Before I can move, he snatches the phone from my hand.

"Hey," I protest, making a grab for it.

Devlin smirks down at me, holding the phone out of my reach. His eyes aren't laughing, though. They're filled with pure loathing. "What the fuck is your family's problem?"

"Right now? You're our problem."

"You're right about that," he says, his jaw tense.

"Give me my phone back," I say, holding out a hand.

"You don't give the orders around here," he says. "Tell me, little doggy. What's their game?"

I cross my arms over my chest, glancing around. There are still dozens of people milling around—a mom with a stroller is struggling to get through the bathroom door, several unattended kids are running in circles screaming, and lots of students stand around talking. I'm not stupid enough to hang out alone, and it comforts me to see all the witnesses if Devlin tries anything. His murderous glare makes every instinct in my brain scream for me to run.

But oh my god… One whiff of his masculine scent gives my body completely different ideas.

"Surely you've figured it out by now," I say, raising my chin and refusing to drop his gaze. "Their game is to take your place. And Dolces always get what they want."

"Do they?" Devlin asks, his smirk returning as his eyes rake down my body, peeling my clothes off with one stroke.

I've never been looked at with such naked lust, and to my horror, my nipples harden at the attention. Hoping he doesn't notice, I force myself to keep up the defensive stance and not cover my chest. "Don't take it personally. We were born to rule. It's in our names."

"Everything is personal," Devlin says, his silky voice dropping as he steps closer, leaning his elbow on the wall above my head, his posture caging me in. He's so close I'm drowning in his intoxicating scent. It's all I can do not to close my eyes and inhale him.

He shouldn't even be out here. Even though he's suspended from the game, he was on the bench with the team.

Why isn't he in the locker room? Are they pissed at him because he lost control and got himself suspended? I know the school kisses his ass, but how much do his teammates like him, and how much is simply fear? If my brothers take his place on the team, will they stay loyal to the Darlings and make life hard for my brothers, or will they welcome a change in the status quo and change loyalties the moment they see how good my brothers are?

Shaking away the thoughts, I place my hands on Devlin's chest, shoving him. He doesn't budge. I might as well be shoving the cinderblock wall behind me. "My brothers will be here in a second," I say. "They'll kill you if they see you this close to me."

"I'm not stupid," he says. "Your brothers won't be looking for you for a very long time, Sweetie Pie. And while they're busy trying to fuck up my life, I'm going to fuck up theirs."

Heart thudding, I duck under his arm and take off. But before I've taken three steps, his hand clamps around the back of my neck. I yelp in pain, and a few people cast curious glances our way. Devlin steers me away from the stadium toward the parking lot.

"Let me go," I yell, hoping to draw enough attention that someone will interfere. I yank to free myself, but Devlin's long fingers crush into my neck, leaving me gasping in pain.

"Be a good dog and shut the fuck up," Devlin growls behind me.

I twist out of his grasp and dash forward, but the moment I hit the parking lot, Preston appears out of nowhere. I slam into him before I can stop myself, and his arms clamp around me like a straitjacket. I scream and kick out, the toes of my shoes beating at his shins. He grunts and shoves me backwards into Devlin's waiting arms.

I scream again, but no one moves to help me. A couple hurries by, pulling their kid to the other side like we might hurt her. Another woman shakes her head like we're just a bunch of annoying teenagers being too loud. The kids I recognize from Willow Heights trail along after us, watching with excitement like they can't wait to see what happens next. Not one person looks surprised. This is either a regular occurrence, a premeditated attack, or both.

"Be a good dog and quit your yapping," Preston says, leaning into my face with a malicious glint in his eye. "Or someone's going to get hurt."

Devlin's hand covers my mouth, and he steers me through the parking lot to a little red convertible. He pulls open the back door, pushing me forward onto the seat. Blind panic rips through me, and I jump up to run. He grabs me, catching my shirt. I hear a tearing sound and feel the chill of the night against my bare skin, but I don't look down. Laughter meets my ears as I give the crowd the show they came for.

Devlin grabs my arm and shoves me back into the car, fury blazing in his blue eyes. "Bad dog," he growls. "All I ask is obedience."

I twist around to crawl across the seat, but he grabs my legs and pulls me back. I kick out, feeling a swell of satisfaction when my foot hits his face—hard.

"A bad dog gets punished," Preston sings above me, and I realize he's circled the car and is standing at the other door.

No escape.

Whatever triumph I felt at kicking Devlin is gone when I hear his belt buckle clinking as he unbuckles. I scream again, fear jolting down my spine like an ice pick.

"Now look what you've gone and done," says a familiar voice. Colt.

I'm jerked back from the feeling of betrayal by the sweep of leather against denim as Devlin yanks his belt free. My mind goes blank with panic, but it's quickly returned to the present by the sting of pain when his belt slaps my ass. I hear it whistle through the air before it cracks against my other ass cheek. A jolt of sharp, stinging pain rushes through me, along with something much more humiliating. His fist knots into my shirt in the center of my back, holding me down while the leather of his belt bites against my jeans again and again.

"Get 'er done!" Preston's mocking voice invades my mind. At least two dozen people have gathered around the car, laughing and cheering as Devlin spanks me with his belt.

Just as suddenly as it began, Devlin's off me. I scramble up on the seat, turning to face my attacker. He stumbles back from the car, breathing hard, ragged, almost like a sob. His eyes are wide and wild, and that scares me more than the rage I saw there earlier.

"My brothers will kill you," I manage, my voice quavering. I still can't comprehend what just happened. I push myself all the way across the seat until my back is pressed against the far door of the convertible. The cold on my cheeks tell me that tears are spilling from my eyes, but I can't feel them. I can't feel anything.

"No, they won't," Colt says, stepping up beside his cousin. "Because you're going to text them that you're okay."

He flashes a lazy grin at me, holding up a phone. My phone.

"Good luck figuring out my password," I shoot back. Fuck Colt and his fake ass. He acted like we were friends, but I see now how stupid I was. It was all part of their plan. Lure me into complacency, let me think this Darling Dog thing wasn't a big deal, and then attack. Whatever fucked up initiation prank this is, I've had enough of it.

"We won't have to guess your password," Preston's silky voice purrs behind me, and his arm snakes around my neck. A flick of his thumb, and a six-inch blade slicks out.

SELENA

"We're going to a party to show off our new pet, and you're going to behave yourself. Aren't you, Sweetie Pie?" Devlin says, hopping over the edge of the door. He straddles my hips, lifting my chin and smiling down at me while his cousin holds a blade just inches from my cheek.

"A party?" I ask, an incredulous laugh forcing its way out. "You're holding a knife to my throat. You just beat me with a belt."

"I bet you liked it," Preston whispers against my ear. His breath is hot against my skin, and a warm chill races through me when Devlin's thumb traces my bare collarbone. What the fuck is wrong with me? This guy has a knife to my throat. But he also has a point. Some sick little part of me thrilled at the helplessness and even the pain of Devlin's punishment. Some part of me that knows I deserved it. That I deserve worse.

"Now, you're going to tell us the password on your phone, or he's going to carve the words *Bad Dog* into your forehead." Devlin's thumb slowly skims over my lower lip, his eyes almost tender as he threatens me.

Preston's breath caresses my neck, his lips brushing the shell of my ear as he lets out a silent laugh. I'm trapped between two purely psychotic boys. Devlin's eyes glitter with malice as he watches me, waiting for my answer, my obedience.

"You're sick," I say, my voice trembling.

"I warned you, baby girl," he says, leaning forward until his nose touches mine. "I'm sicker than you can imagine. Sick enough that I won't care what they do to me. Try to arrest me, sweetheart. I'll be free in an hour, just like last time. And you'll wear my words for the rest of your life. All the plastic surgery in the world won't fix what I'll do to your face."

"Okay," I whisper, clutching Preston's wrist, trying to get the knife away from me. "Don't mark me."

"Oh, it's too late for that," Devlin whispers back. "You might not see it, but I've already marked you, Dolce. You're mine now. And I'm going to have some fun with you tonight."

I start to move, ready to shove him away and fight like hell, but Preston presses the flat side of the blade to my cheek, letting me feel the cold steel like a promise.

"Are you going to be a good doggy?" he purrs in my ear. "Or are you going to make me cut you?"

"Don't cut me," I gasp out.

"Then let's have the password," Colt says, his grinning face appearing over mine so he looks upside down to me, like a freaky funhouse clown.

I whisper the numbers, and he punches them into my phone and then steps back, out of my line of sight.

"Good dog," Devlin says, a triumphant smile twitching at the corners of his lips. He leans down, his lids dropping almost closed as he eyes my lips. Our mouths are so close I can feel the heat of his against mine like a kiss. I can feel it, and the fucked up part is that I almost want it. I want—no, I need—comfort, some release from what's just happened so badly that I'd almost take it from the one who inflicted it. My lids drop closed, and I feel Devlin's mint breath tingle over my skin before he lets out a low chuckle.

"This one's going to take some training," he says, hopping up and sliding into the front seat. "You know what to do with her."

Before I can protest, Preston hauls me over the door of the car, and Colt lifts the lid to the trunk.

"Are you fucking kidding me?" I ask, grinding my heels into the pavement. I twist and wrench at his grip, but I only manage to rip my shirt all the way down the front. I'm fighting too hard to care that my bra is exposed for the entire crowd to see. But I'm no match for these two strong football players. I can't break free. Too soon, I'm stuffed into the trunk and closed in.

I try to breathe. Try not to flip the fuck out. I'm not buried alive. I'm in a car. But the thought of Destiny, the girl who died at one of Devlin's parties, plants itself in my mind. Maybe he was at her grave mourning. Maybe he regrets it as much as I regret the things I did to that girl in Manhattan. But the difference is that I'm trying. I want to be better. Devlin didn't learn a lesson from that. He's still bullying. Still partying. Still stuffing me in a trunk like he put that girl in an early grave, however unintentionally.

Everything in me says to go berserk, that I'm about to die. But they're not taking me somewhere to kill me and dump my body. They're taking me to a party. I won't take dares here. I won't jump off the balcony. I close my eyes, pretend I'm lying in the back seat, that I'm fine. That I'm going to a party to have fun.

If I stop fighting, maybe they'll get bored. They're not going to kill me. They're not. They want to humiliate me the way I humiliated that girl last year. If she could take it all those months, I can take it one night. It won't kill me. They'll have their fun, and they'll let me go. I just have to play along. One thing's for sure. If I had any qualms about taking down these psychos, they're gone now.

The lines are drawn for me now, too. My brothers and the Darlings already drew those lines, but I thought that somehow, if I straddled the line, I didn't have to commit. I thought maybe it wasn't black and white, that maybe my brothers aren't saints and the Darlings aren't devils. I tried to choose good, but I was a fool all along. I'm part of this family feud whether or not I want to be. I always have been. I'm part of it because Dolce blood runs through my veins, and it always will. My only choice is whether to fight for my family or give up.

I didn't stand up for Veronica's victim last year. I let her become mine, too, because I couldn't stand up for myself. This time, I'll stand up. For my family, and for myself.

The car grinds to a stop on gravel, and my heart thuds painfully against my ribs. A second later, the car doors slam, rocking the vehicle.

I'm not going to die, I remind myself. Their footsteps sound on the gravel, and the trunk pops open. Preston stands over me, his switchblade already in his hand. I know when to fight back and when to play along. I'm not going to throw myself on his blade to prove how tough I am.

"Looks like the ride did her good," Devlin says, holding out a hand.

I want to slap his hand away, to punch him in the face. But I hold myself in check and let him help me out of the trunk.

"Ready to be an obedient doggy?" Colt asks, grinning like this is all some hilarious joke.

I nod, but it doesn't matter if they have my agreement. Devlin has already slid something around my neck. I reach up, grabbing it, but he snaps it closed. A second later, he clips a leash into the ring on the front of the leather dog collar. Preston starts laughing.

I cross my arms over my chest, pulling my shirt closed in the process. "I'm not going to a party like this."

"I think you are," Devlin says.

"Be a good dog, and he'll be a good master," Colt says, still smiling like we're all having fun here.

"You fucked with the wrong family," Devlin says. "Let this be a lesson to you. Afterwards, you can go home and tell your brothers all about it."

It strikes me then that they didn't do this in the parking lot impulsively. They weren't in a fit of rage because my brothers got to show off for the coaches and try to replace them. This was premeditated. Calculated. They could have taken me somewhere private, assaulted and murdered me. But they chose a public shaming. Like they said, this is personal. They're sending a message to my family. The Darlings are untouchable. They can get away with murder, but they're sparing us—this time.

"Come on, little doggie," Preston says, slapping his thigh like I'm an actual dog. He steps forward and grabs the tatters of my shirt, wrenching it from me in one violent motion.

"What the fuck," I snap. "Give me your shirt."

"Yeah, right," Colt drawls. "And miss that view? Damn, girl. You got some tits on you."

I watch Devlin's eyes drop to my chest, his Adam's apple bobbing when he swallows. The lights from the house illuminate the globes of my breasts, my olive skin gleaming in the faint glow above the full cups of my pink silk bra.

After a second, Devlin tears his eyes away and turns, giving the leash a yank. Preston and Colt follow me, ready to catch me if I get any ideas about escape. My heart hammers so hard I'm afraid I'll pass out with each step, but I force my legs to keep moving. We start toward the house, an oversized grey stone thing. Unlike our house, this one is modern and not located in a neighborhood. I can hear music pulsing from the house, but there are no neighbors to call the cops if things get loud. No one to hear me if I scream.

There's nothing but fields behind the house, and in the distance, trees. I take a deep breath and tell myself that I will make it through this night. It won't kill me. I will endure whatever they throw at me. I will endure the humiliation. The pain. The shame. As we step onto the front porch, adrenaline races through me, and I feel like I'm about to faint. I've never even taken my shirt off voluntarily for a guy, and now half the school is about to see me without one. With each pull of the leash, I can feel the spikes of the leather dog collar like the one Dixie wore the day I took her place. Now that I'm standing outside a party with a bunch of sociopaths who have me topless and on a fucking leash, that seems like about the worst decision I've ever made.

eighteen

Devlin opens the door without knocking, and I grit my teeth and follow him like an obedient puppy, which is at once humiliating and laughable. Suddenly, I want nothing more than to tell him who I was, who I am. What I've done. I'm no obedient puppy. I'm not cute or sweet or anything of the sort. I'm a fucked up girl in need of psychological help, but I've never rolled over before, and it doesn't come easy now. I keep reminding myself I'm doing this for my family. I won't grovel, won't make a scene like the Darlings want. I will keep my dignity even in the most undignified circumstances.

And while I'm at it, I will find out something that can destroy the Darlings, and I will put an end to these fuckers. If

I fight, I'll not only make the scene worse, but these guys will cut me. I have no doubt that Preston would be true to his word—and that he'd enjoy every second of my torment. That would damage me more than this party ever could.

"Hey," Devlin barks over the noise in the room. People fall silent, turning to gawk at me. Lacey and a couple friends snort with suppressed laughter and look at me like I'm an infectious disease instead of a hot girl in jeans and a three-hundred dollar bra.

Well, fuck them. If I have to wear this shit, I'll strut what I've got. When Devlin pulls me past her, I keep my head high and stroll by like I'm the queen of this fucking party.

When we've passed, I hear the laughter, the shrieks of derision and scorn from Lacey and her cheer bitches. But I don't hate them for it. I *was* those girls. I know what sad lives they have. The fear, the constant paranoia about who's a friend and who will put a knife in your back the second it's turned. I know the powerlessness that makes you have to cut someone else to the bone to feel powerful again. To feel like you have control.

The worst part isn't the taunts. The worst part is when Devlin steps into the kitchen. A keg is set up, and he pulls me over to it and holds out a cup. While someone fills it, two pimply guys laugh and whistle at me. One of them grabs my side, his damp fingers cutting into my bare skin.

I elbow him so hard I hope I crack a bone in his wrist. "Touch me again and fucking die," I say.

Devlin jerks me back, nearly giving me whiplash. I think he's about to get up in my face, but instead, he towers over the groper like he's about to beat his ass. "No one pets the Darling Dog without asking," he thunders.

The kid scurries away, but another guy finishes filling his cup and sidles over to take his place.

"She's so much hotter than the last one," he says. "Can I pet her?"

"Yes," Devlin says, nodding for him to go ahead. The guy's hand goes right for my boob, giving it a squeeze before I slap it away with all the fury I possess.

"Damn," he says, shaking his fingers. "She's mean."

Colt and Preston crack up, but Devlin barely cracks a smile. "She's not trained yet."

I expect Devlin to drink like King, with deliberateness that keeps a drink in his hand at all times but never lets him get out of control. Instead, he chugs his beer and takes another and then another, drinking like he has a death wish and tonight it's coming true.

I can't feel for him, though. Not when he proceeds to parade me around the party letting guys touch me and laughing as I slap the shit out of them. When that gets old, he drags me back to a patio where people are shooting pool and taking shots along an outdoor wooden bar. Music and light spill out into the yard. We lost the other two Darlings, but now I catch sight of Preston supporting a girl who's staggering so badly she can barely keep her feet as they make their way out into the darkness of the yard. Suddenly, fear clenches in my belly.

I've been enduring this night, telling myself over and over that I just have to get through it. But what then? Devlin is drunk as fuck, Preston is clearly a sociopath, and Colt... I have no idea where he is or what he's capable of.

That's when I spot two adults lounging on plush recliners beside the bar, each with a drink in one hand. They're wearing matching robes and observing with an air of keen interest. My heart lurches in my chest, and I cross my arms over myself, trying to cover up for the first time since this started. Maybe they can help me, put a stop to this insanity.

"My, my," the woman drawls as Devlin leads me to the bar. "What do we have here?"

"This is my new dog," Devlin says. "Don't worry, she's house broken."

The woman throws back her head and titters with laughter.

"The things you boys come up with," says the man, shaking his head with an indulgent smile.

No fucking way. That's all they're going to say?

But I must have been delusional to think they'd help me. They're letting a hundred minors drink in their house.

The couple looks about my parents' age, but any similarity ends there. Mom might be a bit of a lush, but she'd never appear in public in a robe, and she only wears makeup to enhance her natural beauty. This woman wears a full face of makeup and a blonde updo with what looks like enough hairspray to hold up the entire decade of the 80s. The man looks about the same age, with a full head of blond hair and the kind of sagging look that men get when they were bulky with muscle and then stop working out and the muscle turns to something else.

Devlin leans on the bar, but the man speaks again. "You'd better keep that one on a shorter leash," he says. "She's a different breed than that one you had over last month."

"The way he goes through them," the woman says. "Just like his father."

My mind latches onto that. So this house isn't some random person's. Her comment makes it sound like she knows his father well… Maybe intimately. Or siblings? Now the lack of knocking makes sense. This must be Colt or Preston's house.

But so what? Okay, so his dad's a philanderer. Half the people our parents know are cheating on their spouses. Not exactly a weapon that will help me take them down.

"You know what I always say, Dev," the man says, waving his drink lazily. "Never trust a beautiful woman. Learned that from your mama." He puts an arm around the woman and kisses her temple, and she squeals with protest and bats at him, giggling.

His mother. Well, I wasn't exactly planning to meet anyone's parents in this get-up, but it's always nice to make a first impression.

They must catch my surprise even through their flirting, because the man laughs and holds up his glass toward me. "What, Devlin didn't tell you about our little wife swap?"

Devlin turns to the man, fury burning in his unfocused eyes that makes me cringe again. Sober, pissed off Devlin is a monster, and I don't want to meet drunk, pissed off Devlin.

"She's a *dog*," he says, his tone withering. "I don't talk to her about our fucked up family."

"Hon-ey," his mom says, but he ignores her, winding the leash around his hand and pulling me away from them. She makes no move to get up and follow, even though Devlin stops fifteen feet away, at the other end of the bar. He's holding me so close I can smell the whiskey on his breath.

"Oh, now you're going to shorten my leash?" I growl. "What do you think's going to happen? Some random guys might want to feel me up? Oh, wait, you've been letting them do that all fucking night."

"I've been *letting* them," he says with a smirk, leaning his elbow on the bar. "I don't mind sharing on occasion as long as they remember who you belong to at the end of the night."

I roll my eyes at his cliché response. "Bullshit," I say. "You didn't give a shit who grabbed me. You let me fend for myself with those assholes. But now you're going to get all possessive because your mom dumped your cheating dad for that guy."

Devlin turns to the bar, and I want to scream in frustration that I can't see his face, can't see his reaction. But I must have hit a nerve to make him hide it from me.

A second later, her turns and shoves a shot into my hand. "Drink."

"No fucking way," I snap.

He takes his shot and slams his glass down on the bar, his slightly unfocused eyes locked on mine. "Wrong. Answer."

Someone fills his shot glass, and he picks it up again and waits.

"I played your insane little game all night," I say. "I let your sleazy friends grope me and feel me up. I walked around on your leash like a good little doggie. I'm not getting drunk with you."

"Yes," he says slowly, a sloppy smile forming on his lips. "I think you are."

"You can't force me to drink."

His hand shoots out and grabs my jaw, his fingers crushing into my cheeks. It hurts like a hammer to the funny bone. I cry out, the shot dropping from my hand as I hit him without thought, an instinctive response to the pain. Devlin's eyes are blind with fury as he shoves my head back and dumps his shot into my mouth.

The familiar sweet tang of whiskey invades my mouth and nose. I've drank before. Not a lot, and I don't like it, but I've snuck drinks from the liquor cabinet, even gotten drunk with Veronica. But there's no way I'm losing control and acting the fool at a party where I've already walked around topless on a leash.

Devlin releases his grip, and I spit a stream of whiskey right in his face. He stumbles back, blinking the burning liquid from his eyes.

"You fucking cunt," he says, jerking the leash so hard I stumble forward. He shoves me down, my hands and knees hitting the wooden deck. He rolls me over and jumps onto me, his powerful thighs caging my torso as he sits on my belly.

"Let me go, you psycho," I scream. Before I can think about it, I pull back and slap his face as hard as I can, my palm stinging with the force of the blow.

Devlin's palm cracks across my cheek, whipping my head sideways. I'm too stunned to do anything but fight back blindly, without strategy, which does nothing but tire me out. My body is no match for Devlin's muscular one sitting astride it. Devlin pins my arms to the deck before lifting his head and bellowing, "Preston!"

When no response comes, Devlin looks around at the group gathered to watch our scuffle.

"Give me a knife," he says. "This bitch doesn't know when to quit."

"No," I cry, going still under him. "Don't cut me."

"You were warned," he growls. "Behave at the party or get a permanent reminder of who you belong to. Think of it like a dog tag you can never take off."

"Please don't cut me," I blurt as someone hands him a pocket knife. I grab his wrist, but he forces my hand down until the tip of the blade touches my forehead. My body is suddenly shaking, fear coursing through me with each heartbeat. "Please," I beg. "I'll do what you want. I'll do anything you want. I'll be obedient. I'll drink all the shots you give me."

Devlin leans down, his expression regretful as he strokes his fingers gently across my cheek, tucking my hair behind my ear. "Good dog," he whispers, and he chucks me under the chin like I really am a fucking dog.

He hands the knife back and pulls me to my feet, wrapping an arm around my waist. His fingers are cool against my bare skin, and I try to ignore the heat spreading where he touches. God, how can I still be attracted to this boy? How can I hate him and want him at the same time?

He hands me a shot and clinks his own against it. I'm tempted to throw the drink in his face and try to run again, but I know when I'm beaten. Gathering my last shred of dignity, I take the shot without wincing at the burn.

"A girl who can throw down whiskey," Devlin purrs, nuzzling my ear. "I like it."

A hot chill races through me, and I tell myself that I won't give in to what my body wants no matter how drunk I get. But I'm terrified that if I take enough shots, I'll forget how much I hate him. Once he's fed me a few shots, though, he seems to grow bored of it. I'm not fighting him anymore, so I'm no fun. He obviously likes the challenge. The luster of having a new pet has worn off now that he's shown me off to everyone at the party and gotten my complete obedience.

The more I know him, the harder it is to hate him, even when he's stumbling around the party with his arm around me, so drunk I don't know if I'm holding him up or being his dog. I haven't gotten any information that can take down the Darlings, but I know a lot more about Devlin Darling. His mother is a lush, and no matter how badly he acts, she won't say no to him. And neither will anyone else. He has more power than he knows what to do with.

At last, he sees Colt and throws an arm around him. "Let's get out of here," he slurs. "This party is dead."

I want to point out that it's his party, but I keep my mouth shut because I want to get out of here, too. Devlin is drunk off his ass, and I have no idea what he'll come up with next. Since his aim seems to be public shaming, it's safer to have him somewhere without an audience.

When we reach the car, Devlin tries to get in the driver's seat, and panic clutches me. I grab his arm. "Let me drive."

Devlin looks down at me like he forgot I was on the end of his leash. "Sweetie Pie," he says with a slur, stepping closer to me. He drops the leash and cups my face in his large palms, his eyes struggling to focus on mine, his breath so whiskey-soaked it could get me drunk. At least, I blame that for the lightheadedness that makes my head swim when his hips crowd mine against the sleek car, rocking slightly and sending a curl of pleasure through my traitorous body.

His fingers slide behind my neck, his gaze sweeping over my face to my full lips. My heart stops. He's going to kiss me.

A soft snapping sound startles me, and I feel the collar release from my neck.

Devlin smirks. "I may be drunk, but I'd have to be dead in a ditch before I let a dog drive my car."

"Fine," I say, shoving at his chest. "Kill yourself. I don't care."

He doesn't even budge. He smiles wider, slowly rocking his hips against mine, his neck arched to look down into my face. "We're gonna fuck, aren't we?"

"Get off me," I say, flustered by the physical contact and the way my body is doing things I definitely didn't give it permission to do.

Devlin's fingers skim my cheek before he buries them in my hair, tugging gently to tip my head back. "Come with me," he says, his words impulsive but sincere for once, and I see a flash of the Devlin girls must fall for. Tortured, fucked up, *passionate.* The fire of rage I saw earlier has been tempered by alcohol, and now he's looking at me with a ravenous hunger, like he needs me so much he might die if I say no. His thumb skims over my full lower lip, and a tingle runs through me, whispering to my own need.

"Say yes," he murmurs, his voice smooth and sweet as cream.

For one terrible second, I forget everything else. Devlin has done something to me, pulled me into the magnetic air around him, made me forget who he is and who I am and what he did to me tonight. And then my brain overrules my dizzy body.

"No." I shove at his chest again, and Devlin takes his sweet time stepping back, making sure I know that he could keep me pinned there if he wanted. That he's letting me go on his terms.

Colt looks back and forth between us, as if waiting to see if we're done. When neither of us speak, he steps up behind Devlin.

"Let me drive," he says, clapping a hand over Devlin's shoulder.

Relieved, I reach for the back door of the car, but Devlin grabs my wrist. "What you doing there, Sweetie?"

I glare at him. "Getting a ride home."

"Maybe next time."

"Are you fucking kidding me?" I demand. "How am I going to get home?"

"Maybe you can take a run," he says, a cruel smile twisting his lips. "Dogs need their exercise."

"I don't know where we are," I point out. "In case you forgot, you drove me here in the trunk of your fucking car."

"Not our problem," Colt says with a wink.

"Dogs are good at finding their way home," Devlin says, climbing into the car.

Colt hops in the car with Devlin, and they speed away into the night and disappear.

nineteen

Only when the guys are gone do I remember that Colt has my phone. Fucking asshole.

I stomp back inside. Everyone's already seen me, so it's not like I have anything to hide. But somehow, I still feel vulnerable walking in alone. When I was with Devlin, I was a prop, an oddity, a circus freak. The girl on a leash. I was a dog, but I was *his* dog. Now, I have no protection. No excuse for being here in my bra. Maybe some small part of me enjoyed the humiliation, or at least knew I deserved it. This is different. Instead of feeling like I'm being shown off, now I just feel like a loser.

I edge up the stairs, looking for a bedroom. I don't care what I put on, I just want to cover myself. A stained old T-shirt would be more than welcome right now. Anything to cover up the amount of skin I'm showing. Guys leer at me as I climb the stairs, but I glare so fiercely that they don't say anything. I'm almost to the top of the stairs when a tall guy grins at me. After a second, I recognize him as the guy Preston forced to eat dog food in the hall.

"Hey, dog," he says. "I'm more of a cat person, but I'll fuck a bitch on occasion."

"Yeah?" I say. "Then go fuck yourself."

I shove past him, but just as I go, I feel his fingers hook under the back of my bra. When I try to twist away, he unhooks it with his other hand. I grab it to my chest and run up the last few steps, my face burning as I listen to the laughter behind me.

After hooking my bra and taking a second to compose myself, I try the door to each room as I pass. The first few are locked. On the third try, the knob turns. I push open the door only to see Preston fucking a girl from behind while she goes down on another girl. Preston's holding a phone, and for a second I think he's scrolling, but when he turns it my way, I realize he's recording it.

"Join the train, Manhattan," he says with a grin. "I can add New York to my list."

I slam the door and hurry to a door that's standing open. I find a bathroom and duck inside. There's not so much as a robe inside. I consider wearing a towel, but at this point, that might draw more attention than my bra. I root through the cabinets and drawers, and just as I'm about to give up, I spot a pack of bobby pins. Like any normal girl, I've picked my share of locks. I pocket a couple and go back into the hall. After listening at the first door, I slip the bobby pin into the lock, feel around until I find the locking mechanism, and pop it open. I slip inside.

The room is dark, but once my eyes adjust, I can see from the light shining in off the balcony that it's also empty. Relief washes over me, and within seconds, I'm in an oversized T-shirt. I've never felt so safe and comforted. I may never wear anything else. The relief seems to weaken me, and I lock the door and then sink onto the edge of the bed. I'm tempted to pass out. I'm a little tipsy, and after the extreme emotional trial of this evening, I'm ready to collapse.

But I don't know whose room this is. I don't know when they'll come in, and what they'd do to me if they found me here. I don't want to think about it, so I drag myself up and step out onto the balcony. A jolt goes through me when I spot a shadow slumped in a patio chair. My mental checklist marks off all the guys I know are dangerous before the figure turns, and I see that it's not a guy at all. It's Dolly.

"Oh, hi," I say, retreating a step.

Dolly's eyes narrow, her fake lashes casting shadows on her cheeks. "Are you in there with Devlin?" Her voice is soft and breathy and sweetly southern.

"No."

She sighs and leans back into her chair again. "Well, at least I won't be stuck out here listenin' to you two fuck all night."

"What?"

"That's Devlin's room," she says, like I should know this. "I was hopin' he'd come in alone, and we could talk. But then I heard someone come in, and I thought, well shit. What if he came in with a girl, and I can't tell them I'm out here without lookin' like a stalker, so I'll just have to listen to him fuckin' her."

"Um. Okay."

"And I know Devlin," she says. "He doesn't do short and sweet. I'd be out here all night listening to you screaming his name like you're trying out for the lead role in a porno flick. It's pretty much my worst nightmare."

"Well, then I guess it's a good thing it didn't happen."

"You know where he's at?"

"He left," I say, crossing my arms over my chest. "I just came up here looking for clothes."

"Oh yeah," she says, glancing at my T-shirt. "He likes that shirt."

"This is Devlin's shirt?"

"Course it is."

I roll my eyes. "Of course I'd have the shitty luck to walk into his room."

"He left you here?"

"Yeah," I say. "He told me to run home. I'm a literal dog to him."

"Oh, yeah," she says. "You are the Darling Dog, aren't you? Sweetie or somethin' like that?"

"Crystal, actually."

"Well, Crystal Actually," she drawls. "Believe it or not, I'd trade places with you in a heartbeat."

I snort at that. "Oh, right. The mayor's daughter wants to be dragged around a party in her bra with a leash around her neck and barked at when she walks by."

"Yeah," she says. "I got it all, don't I?"

"Sorry," I say, feeling shitty for assuming to know anything about her. To her, maybe it really does look like I have it all. Four protective brothers, a wealthy family, and the one thing she really wants—Devlin Darling's undivided attention.

"It's okay," Dolly says glumly. "Everyone thinks that."

"If I could trade with you, I would," I assure her.

She laughs quietly. "No, you wouldn't."

"Well, it's not really an option, so there's no use arguing about it," I say. "I'm sure you have your reasons for wanting Devlin, but trust me when I say that I don't."

"They all say that," she says with a sigh.

"Who? His *dogs?*"

"Yeah," she says. "One of the guys usually throws them a pity fuck as a kind of consolation for all they had to go through. And the thing is, they end up wishing they could be the dog again when their turn is over."

"Wait, were you a Darling Dog?"

"Oh, honey," she says. "Bless your heart."

"Is that a no?"

"Gosh no. I was the original Darling Doll. That's why people call it that. After me." She sits up straight when she says this, as if she's so proud that the Darling boys' groupies are named after her.

"I'm assuming no one can go from Dog to Doll and vice versa."

"Course not," she says. "Though the Dogs keep dreaming one day they will."

"Uh huh," I say. "And what exactly is the difference between one of these *dogs,* who chase after the Darlings wanting to get back their position as whipping boy, and the dolls who chase after them wanting basically the same thing?"

"To the Darlings? There's probably not much difference. I don't know. A Darling Dog might last for a whole year, or a whole semester. A Doll is lucky to get a month or two. I bet you'll know Devlin better than most people when he's done with you."

"And yet, I'll be scum to the rest of the school. Pathetic, worthless trash that he got tired of and threw away. While you get a whole legion of groupies named after you."

"I supposed it's a matter of perceived value," she concedes. "A girl they date has value afterwards. If she's good enough for a Darling, just about any guy wants her. A Dog is all broken when they finish with her. She's forever ruined for other guys."

twenty

A tapping on my window wakes me. I sit up and rub my eyes, my mind heavy with sleep and confusion. It's not even fully light outside. I'm about to lie back down when the tapping sounds again.

What if it wakes my brothers?

Shit. I scramble from the bed and go to the window. Outside, I can see a shadowy figure silhouetted against the bluing sky after dawn.

"Go away," I hiss, but of course he can't hear me. I unlock the window and crack it a few inches.

"What dawn outside yonder window breaks?" he says in a dramatic voice.

"Shhh," I hiss. "And go away."

"Let me in," he says. "I just want to talk."

"You gave up that chance when you ditched me in the middle of nowhere," I say. "You're as bad as the rest of them. Worse. They never pretended to be my friend."

"I'm sorry," he says, giving me some really fucking adorable puppy dog eyes. "Let me in, Fair Verona."

I feel my resolve crumbling as laughter wells inside me. "You know that's the city where they lived in Italy, right?" I say. "It's not a person."

"Whatever," he says. "Let me in, Juliet, or I'll stand out here until it gets light."

"Or I call the cops on you for harassment."

His eyes narrow. "Are you the one who called the cops on the fight?"

"What? No," I protest. "I may be a bitch, but I'm sure as fuck not a rat."

"I didn't think so." He pops the screen from my window in two seconds flat and sticks his hand through the gap.

"What do you want?" I ask.

"I brought your phone back."

I pull open the window, and Colt ducks through and hands me my phone. I snatch it and then cross my arms over my chest, only realizing I'm still in Devlin's shirt now that his cousin is standing in my room. "I figured Devlin would be the one to come busting into my room at dawn to torture me some more."

"He's sleeping off last night," Colt says, eyeing my bare legs below my underwear and T-shirt.

I slip back to the bed, pawing some pillows behind me and sitting up with the blankets pulled up to my waist. It feels weird to be talking in the dark, so I switch on the lamp.

Colt glances around my room. "That's a lot of pillows for one person."

"What are you here for, again?" I ask.

"To say I'm sorry about last night."

"Oh," I say, too surprised to have a snarky comeback ready.

"I really do want us to be friends," Colt says, sinking onto the edge of my bed beside me. "I think you're awesome. And not one bit doglike in any sense of the word."

I snort. "Is that what you tell all the girls the morning after you hold a knife to their face and threaten to permanently disfigure them?"

"You know, we really are like Romeo and Juliet," he says, grabbing a handful of pillows off the floor and settling at the foot of my bed with them. "Betraying our families to have the greatest love affair ever known."

"Is that what this is?" I ask. "I thought it was more like your family repeatedly assaulting mine."

"You know that's not what happened," he says, crossing his arms over his chest. I notice he's wearing the same jeans and polo he wore last night. Of course. He drove Devlin home and crashed there.

"You're right," I admit.

"If Devlin hadn't pulled me out of the way, they would have permanently disfigured me," he says. "Or killed me. Your brother wasn't going to slow down just because a person was standing against that car."

I stare at the shape of my legs under the blankets because I can't speak. I haven't wanted to admit that truth even to myself. I refuse to watch the video that everyone else in the school has seen a dozen times, the one with Devlin kicking my brother on the ground. It makes Devlin look like a monster, but that's not the reason I haven't watched it. I haven't watched it because I know what happened off screen, behind the cameras, the parts artfully cut by the photographer. And those parts make my brothers look like monsters.

"What are we going to do?" I whisper.

Colt's hand moves over the top of the blanket until it finds my foot. His fingers close around it and squeeze. "We have to do something," he says. "Before it goes too far."

I nod, swallowing hard. A swell of something light and intoxicating builds in my chest. Hope.

"Okay," I say. "Let's make a truce."

twenty-one

Some people get respect by earning it, by being the best at something like football or by never betraying what's right. Others demand it with fear and intimidation. Some people earn their wealth by starting from nothing and doing what has to be done to make something of themselves. Others rest on their family name, on a fortune earned by the sweat of their grandfathers. They can call me a dog, but I won't bow to the entitled assholes of this world who haven't earned my submission.

"You feeling better?" Royal asks when I walk into the kitchen. My brothers are slouched in chairs along the bar, a plate of picked-over fruit in the center.

"Fine," I say, hopping onto a barstool and snagging a glass of orange juice they left for me.

"Guess what?" Duke asks, a big grin spreading across his face.

"Wait," Royal says, holding up a hand. "How'd you get home?"

I shrug and pop a grape into my mouth. "Dolly gave me a ride."

"You said Dixie's friend was giving you a ride home," Royal says, narrowing his eyes at me. Damn him and his twin instincts, and thank god we don't have twin telepathy, which I swear Duke and Baron do.

"Yeah," I say slowly. "Dixie's friend Dolly." I stare at him like he's crazy even though my heart is hammering. I hate lying to my brothers, especially him. But sometimes it has to be done.

"Dolly Beckett," King says. "The mayor's daughter?"

"Yes," I say, rolling my eyes. "What's with the inquisition? I told you she was giving me a ride home, and she did. End of story."

"Why didn't you just say Dolly was giving you a ride home?" Duke asks. "And by the way, you can let her know she can ride me home any time."

"And that's why I didn't say her name," I say, shaking my head.

"You can't be friends with her," Duke says.

"I'm not."

"Good," he says. "Because I'm not gonna be able to hold up my end of the agreement if she's your friend. I'm sorry, sis, but that ass is just begging for a good Dolce dicking."

"TMI," I say, filling my plate with whatever's left of my brothers' breakfast. "But you should probably clear it with Dad if you're going to pump-and-dump the mayor's daughter. I don't think that'll go over too well with Mayor Perv-o Beckett."

"The mayor can eat my ass," Duke says. "I'm not afraid of him. He's the mayor of what? Thirty thousand people? Oh, gosh, I'm shaking in my boots."

"That clown has no power," King agrees. "It's not like he's the mayor of New York."

"He's already helped us all we needed him to," Baron says, flashing me a grin.

"Wait," I say, dropping my fork. "Really? That's what you were going to tell me?"

"Yep," Duke says, holding up his hand. I slap him five before hopping off the barstool to hug them all.

"We got a tryout," King says, grinning as he lifts me off the floor and spins me around.

"That's amazing," I say honestly. I know how much this means to my brothers. I'm nervous as hell for what I have to do, but maybe they'll take it better now that they're in such a good mood.

"I have some good news, too," I say, resuming my seat. "The Darlings are ready to put all this behind us and make peace."

"I knew we'd break them," Duke says, slapping fives with Baron.

"Who told you that?" Royal asks, his intense, dark eyes fixed on me.

Blood rushes in my head, but I keep my voice even. "Colt."

"When?"

"This morning," I say.

"You gave him your phone number?" Royal asks, his eyes darkening even further.

"Yes." I resist the urge to add more, to say that we have a project together or something else to excuse it.

"Why would you do that?" Royal asks, his hand clenched on the bar. I should have known he'd be the hardest to convince, the one who wouldn't let me off easy. He never has.

"Because I like him," I say. "And he likes me. He asked me to Homecoming tonight, and I said yes."

"This better be a fucking joke," King says.

"It's not," I say, now making shit up on the fly. "In fact, that's where I really went last night. I went to get a dress."

The vein in the side of Royal's temple is throbbing so hard I can see it. Duke looks like his head's about to explode, and Baron is just gaping in utter confusion.

"You're not going to that dance with a Darling," King says, his face reddening and his eyes blazing with anger.

"I know you hate them," I say, holding up both hands. "And if you say I can't go, then I won't. But before you decide that, I want you to hear me out. Okay?"

Royal slams his fist down on the counter. "Fuck. No."

"Come on," I say, rolling my eyes. "I said I wouldn't go if you didn't want me to, even though I really want to."

"Have you been sneaking around with him?" King asks.

"No," I snap. "I wouldn't do that. We've never even kissed."

"You better not have," Duke says.

"Give me a fucking break," I say, my own anger rising. "The four of you have fucked more girls than there are in this entire town, and I can't even think about kissing a boy? I can't have a crush, or buy a pretty dress and go to a dance like every other girl in this country? That's bullshit, and you fucking know it."

"You've been to a dance," Royal says quietly.

"With some lame-ass friend of yours who wouldn't even dance with me because he was afraid you'd kick his ass if he touched my hip," I say. "You guys are my brothers, and I love you, but I'm not five years old. I'm sixteen, and my body doesn't belong to you."

"You already fucked him, didn't you?" Duke asks.

I resist the urge to throw my orange juice in his face. "No, but if I did, it would be none of your business," I snap. "I'm old enough to date, and Colt's nice. If you'd give him a chance, you'd know that."

"You really like him, don't you?" Royal asks, staring at me like I'm a stranger.

"He's funny, and he makes me happy," I say, lifting my chin and refusing to back down, even though the look my twin's giving me crushes my soul. "Besides that, he's going to call off his cousins so they don't get back at you for destroying Devlin's car, which by the way can't be replaced at the dealership like the Range Rover. This stupid out-pranking each other thing isn't funny anymore. You could have killed Colt."

"I wish I had," Royal growls, glowering at me.

"And in return for him doing that," I say. "You're going to drop the charges against him."

"Like hell," Royal says, touching his bruised face.

"And he won't press charges against you for attempted murder," I say, giving him a hard look.

"No way," King says. "He's going to do all that if he wants to talk to our sister."

"There's no point," I say, crossing my arms. "If you're all going to be assholes and hurt him, I won't see him. I'm not going to put him in danger."

"Fuck," Royal says, dropping his head and rubbing the spot between his eyebrows. "You like this guy."

I sigh. "Look, it's about more than whether I like someone. You're all going to be on the team together. And I'm sure you know better than anyone that being on a hostile team that doesn't want you there isn't going to work. They won't play for you if you're responsible for getting their star suspended."

"They will once they see us play," Duke says.

I shake my head. "It doesn't matter if you're just as good. They'll sabotage you. The whole team will boycott. People in the south are different. A name is here is like blood. They're loyal to that."

"She might have a point," King concedes quietly.

My other brothers stare at him. "You're really going to give up?" Duke asks.

"I'm not giving up," King says. "But even if Devlin's off the team for good, the other two are there. And they're good."

I know my brothers well enough to know there's another reason King gave in. He knows I'm right about the pranks. They've gotten dangerous, and if there's one thing stronger than King's pride, it's his protectiveness. He won't say it because he doesn't want to wound any egos, but he doesn't want our brothers to get hurt, either.

"I guess if we're really going to quit, we might as well quit while we're ahead," Duke says. "We hit last."

"And it'll look like they gave in," Baron points out. "We wrecked Devlin's car and got him suspended, and now we're all friends? Looks like they're the ones who broke first."

Royal just glowers at me. I smile at him and hop off my chair. "Well, we didn't find a dress, which means I'm going shopping with Dixie today. I'd better get going."

"Why don't I join you?" Royal says.

"You want to go dress shopping?" I ask, planting a hand on my hip.

"How else are you going to get around?"

"Wouldn't be an issue if I had my license," I sing-song as a reminder.

"No way am I trusting you with a car now," he says.

A shock of hurt hits me with his words, even stronger because that distrust is warranted. It's true that I'm going to Homecoming with Colt, and that he makes me laugh. It's true that I'm going to ask Dixie to go last-minute dress shopping today, not sneaking off to meet Colt for a secret rendezvous as Royal obviously thinks. But there are other lies laced in with the truth, and other schemes behind my words. My side went surprisingly well, but I'm not sure how easily Colt will be able to convince his family.

I go up to my room to shower and message Dixie.

UnsweetDolce: Hey, girl. I might need to invoke the last minute emergency friend favor.

DixieDog: OMG what happened? U ok?

UnsweetDolce: Yes, but I need a dress for tonight.

DixieDog: No way! You're going to HC? With who?

UnsweetDolce: Colt. Don't freak out and say Darling in that creepy way.

DixieDog: Totally freaking out!

UnsweetDolce: Help me find a dress? If not, no prob. My brother's going anyway.

DixieDog: Your brother can't help you dress shop.

UnsweetDolce: Is that a yes? Thank you so much! Sorry it's last minute.

DixieDog: You're saving me from a trip to the country club. I should be thanking you.

An hour later, we pull up outside Dixie's. She comes running out and hops up into the back seat. "I cannot believe Colt Darling asked you to Homecoming," she gushes. "Tell me every single detail."

I glance at Royal, who's grinding his teeth but currently not speaking to me.

"It's not a big deal," I say. "We were just talking, and he asked who I was going with. I told him I wasn't going, and he asked me."

"No way," Dixie squeals. "You're so lucky."

"You're not going?" I ask as the car speeds toward the tiny shopping center in town.

Dixie snorts. "I'm only a freshman. I can't even go alone. They don't allow freshmen unless their date is an upperclassman."

"Royal's a sophomore," I point out.

"Oh... No, it's okay," Dixie says, going red to the roots of her hair. "Really, I'm good. I'll go next year."

"I'll take you," Royal says, breaking his silence at last.

"You don't have to," Dixie mumbles.

"Okay," Royal says. "If you don't want to go, I won't take you."

"I mean, I want to," she blurts, blushing even harder. "But you probably have someone you'd rather ask."

"You can just go as friends if it makes you more comfortable," I say. "Like me and Colt."

I catch Royal's eye, and seeing the relief there lets me know I did the right thing. I want him to be okay with the Darlings, but I don't want to upset him. If it makes him happy, I'll go as friends with Colt. I'm not even sure I like Colt. Sometimes he's great, and other times… Not so much.

"Okay," Dixie says. "But, I mean, don't you guys already have dates?"

I roll my eyes and turn to my friend in the back seat. "When a cute boy asks you out, and you want to go, the answer you usually give is *yes.*"

"Yes," she whispers.

"Great," I say. "Now, let's go get some dresses."

twenty-two

So this is how reconciliation feels. Despite my brothers' misgivings, I feel good. Taking down the Darlings never felt quite right to me. But joining them at the top, sharing their throne, and making sure I use that power to protect people—that feels right. Having a say in it, and not just doing what my family wants, that feels right. For the first time in a long time, I might be able to do something for me, too, not just the Dolce name. And that's the kind of power I want.

"This limo is tacky as fuck," I say, laughing as I climb in next to Dixie and Dolly, who by some miracle agreed to be Duke's date. I thought she might be with Preston now, but obviously she's got better taste than I gave her credit for. I almost feel bad for her. The poor girl has no idea what's about to hit her. My brothers may be loyal to me, but that trait doesn't carry over into their dating lives.

Baron quietly asked a cheerleader sometime in the past month, and we're all riding together. Once the girls are in, Duke and Baron squeeze in next to their dates. Royal stands glaring at Colt, who ducks in next to me before my brother relents and climbs in.

"I'd so kiss you if your brother wasn't here right now," Colt says to me with a grin.

"And if we were going as more than friends," I remind him. I made the concession to appease Royal, who was royally pissed about the whole thing, but I also don't want Colt to get the wrong impression. We made up the whole star-crossed lovers thing to get our families to drop their feud, but it's hard to tell with Colt when he's serious and when he's not. I don't want to lead him on when I'm not really sure how I feel about him. My heart doesn't stutter step when someone mentions his name, and his smell doesn't make me dizzy no matter how deeply I inhale it. But he's fun when he's not following his psycho cousins, who are banned from the dance along with King.

"Let's get this party started," Duke says, grabbing some champagne while Dixie hands out glasses, giggling all the while. We crank up the music and open the top of the limo while it speeds down the road toward the swanky club where the dance is being held. Duke opens the champagne, making sure to spray some on Dolly so he can lick it off her cleavage while she yelps in surprise. She doesn't look exactly appalled, though. Most girls don't see Duke coming until it's too late, until they're seeing his taillights as he's going.

"I've never been in a limo," Dixie shouts over the music, her cheeks flushed from the little bit of champagne she's had.

"Then you have to get out the top," I yell back. "Come on. I'll go with you."

We both stand and stick our heads out, yelling into the chilly October night and holding our arms up like we're on a rollercoaster.

"Someone's slapping my ass," she shrieks, doing a funny little dance step before collapsing back inside in a heap of giggles.

"Come back in," Dolly yells. "You're gonna mess up your hair."

"I don't care."

For one moment, I stay out there alone. I open my mouth wide and scream, then inhale, swallowing up the whole night. The cold, the sparse lights in the small town, the cars driving by with flags for the school, the laughter of my friends inside, the buzz of champagne bubbling in my veins. I feel electric.

When we get to the dance, we've already polished off three bottles of champagne, and we're all a little tipsy. The people taking tickets give us dirty looks that range from suspicious to disgusted to pissed, but we don't care. We brought the party.

I realize that as we step into the dance hall, beautifully decorated with black and gold. A swarm descends on Colt, and no one seems to remember that Dixie and I were Dolce dogs. We have beautiful boys on our arms. We laugh as loud as we want to. We dance before anyone's dancing because we can.

Yeah, Lacey and her bitchy friends stand at the edge of the dance floor giving us looks and snickering, but I know it's only because they're not confident enough to walk out onto an empty dance floor and kick things off. That's okay. Someone's gotta do it.

And pretty soon, other people come out and dance with us, and then the dance floor is full. People might say they hate the social hierarchy, but they don't. The truth is, we created it, and without it, no one would know where they fit. And everyone likes to fit somewhere. What they like even more is knowing where everyone else fits. When we're like this, people are comfortable. No one wonders where we fit; no one is on edge because they don't know what to do with us. We belong with the Darlings, at the top. That's something they understand.

Colt dances up close to me, lifting his arms and swiveling his hips. "This colt hasn't been broken," he says, giving me that sexy, young-Matthew McConaughey grin. "Wanna try riding this one bareback, or do you need a saddle?"

"I need a lot more alcohol," I say, laughing and moving in time with him, leaving a space between us.

"That can be arranged," Colt says, hooking an arm around my waist and pulling me to him. He pushes his thigh between mine and moves in a slower, dirtier rhythm. "You sure about this just-friends thing?" he asks, his champagne breath warming my cheeks. "Because I'm feeling something."

"It's called drunk," I say, pushing lightly against his chest.

"Is it?" he asks, his lips brushing my cheek and sending a shiver down my spine. He takes my hand and brings it between us, pressing my palm against a rigid bulge in his pants. I'm so shocked I wrap my fingers around his shaft without thought. I've never touched a guy like this before, and my heart stammers in my chest at the intimate contact. Before my brain catches up to my body, Colt's lips meet mine. He pushes his hard-on into my hand, groaning into my mouth and plunging his tongue between my lips.

"Colt," I say, tearing my lips away and jerking my hand from his. "What are you doing? We're in the middle of a room full of people."

He catches my hand, grinning and giving me his puppy-dog eyes. "We can go somewhere more private if you want."

"I don't," I say, my body rigid in his grip. "I said we were just going as friends."

"To make your brother happy," he says. "He doesn't have to know it's more than that."

"It's not," I say, convinced of the truth of my own words now that I've spoken. Sure, it felt good, and the memory of his thickness in my fingers sends a dart of excitement through me. If I'd never stood waiting for Devlin's lips to meet mine, the whole world spinning upside down and out of control, Colt's kiss might have been enough. If I'd never felt Devlin's breath against my lips and prayed so hard for him to kiss me that there was not a single thought in my head, it might have. If I'd never felt my knees buckle at the scent of his skin, it might.

But I have. Colt's touch is nice, but it's not Devlin's. I find my eyes straying to the door, but of course he's not here. He can't come to this.

"Okay," Colt says with a shrug and a lazy grin. "If you say so."

And then he keeps on dancing like I didn't just shoot him down. I can't tell if he's really unaffected, or if he hides it as well as he hides everything else.

"Let's just have fun," I say.

"Already having it," Colt says, spinning me around and pinning me to his chest, his hips grinding into mine. I like dancing, and if he's okay with dancing with me after I rejected him, then I'm okay with it, too. Maybe he goes around kissing girls all the time. On my first day, Lacey told me to watch out for him and Preston, that they go through girls like tissues and toss them away with as little thought. I have to believe Colt is just doing what he does, that he'll just find some other girl for his next victim as easily as he found me.

We dance, and after a while, the awkwardness is forgotten. I dance with the girls, and in a group with everyone, and jump up and down with my brothers to an energetic song. Dolly has no shame and does the chicken dance to some song, so I join her. When Lacey and her bitchy friends start mocking us, Dolly just yells for me to "shake my tail feathers at them." She turns out to be lots of fun, despite her gloomy disposition the night before. I don't even care if I'm a Dog or a Doll or neither or both. I just care that I have friends to dance with, the feud is over, and I'm having fun. Everything is perfect.

We've been dancing for a few hours when suddenly, a hush falls over the dance floor. I turn, searching for the commotion. One of the doormen is at the DJ booth, gesturing angrily. I feel a prickle on the back of my neck and turn slowly. Devlin Darling stands at the edge of the dance floor in dark jeans and a buttoned shirt, staring at me.

With a scratch, the music dies.

The dancers grumble, then fall silent when they realize there's drama to witness.

Or… Something.

My heart hammers so hard that I can't think of or feel anything else. I join the crowd in gaping at Devlin. He gives a quick glance around and then strides forward. Toward me. The girl he humiliated and threatened last night. The girl he called a dog, and forced to take shots, and led around a party on a leash like a fucking animal.

He stops in front of me. I should cringe away from him, but I don't. I inhale the clean soapy smell of him, like he just showered. His hair is combed back and looks still wet. His skin is smoothly shaven. His blue eyes pierce into mine, down to my very soul.

He holds out a hand. "Dance with me."

I can't think of the right response. My mouth opens, and words pop out. "You're not supposed to be here."

"One dance," he says, stepping forward so we're close enough to dance. All I have to do is put my hand in his. I look at his lips, so tempting they make my mouth water. But I don't move.

"Why?" I whisper, suddenly short of breath.

"I came here for one dance," he says. "Then I'll leave."

"I don't think they're going to let you stay for even one dance."

"They can try to throw me out," he says. "But I'm not leaving until I've danced with you."

"You'll get arrested again."

"It'll be worth it."

I swallow hard before sliding my arms around his neck. His hands fall gently on my hips. The DJ starts the music, a different song now—"Say You Won't Let Go."

"How did you know I like this song?" I whisper against his ear.

Devlin shudders and pulls me closer, his eyes dropping closed for a second. "Lucky guess."

"Or gross invasion of privacy?"

"Yeah, that too."

I lay my head on his chest, angling my mouth up toward his neck. "Devlin? Why are you really here?"

"I don't know," he admits. "I was at home, and everything was fine. But I couldn't stop thinking about you here with my cousin. It was fucking with my head. I got tired of being pissed about it, so I came here to see what you were doing."

"Wow," I say, laughing shakily. "Stalk much?"

"When it's you? Fuck yes."

"But you hate me."

"So?" he says. "You hate me, too."

We stare at each other for a long moment. I search his eyes, finding a challenge there, as if he thinks I'll contradict him. I swallow hard and then nod. "Yeah…"

"Then shut up and dance with me until the cops come."

His hands are strong on my waist, his long fingers almost circling my middle and making me feel small and fragile. His body is hard against mine, sending my pulse racing and my brain spiraling as I inhale against his neck. For one moment, for one song, I let myself go. I let myself imagine what it would be like, this fairytale. I let myself believe.

And then the song ends, and Devlin pulls back. He stares into my eyes, neither of us letting go. The music changes to something that requires twerking and grinding, but Devlin's eyes never leave mine, his hands still on my waist, his hips barely swaying. My pulse begins to pound hard and slow. I'm barely moving, but my breath comes faster than if I was dancing my heart out.

"Devlin," I say slowly.

And then a commotion at the door draws our attention. Someone shrieks, and a ripple of voices spreads across the room.

"Cops..."

"Cops..."

"Cops—"

"I better go," Devlin says, the corner of his mouth quirking for just a second.

"I thought you were untouchable," I say. "You can't even bully your way into a school dance?"

Colt grabs Devlin's arm and my hand, dragging us toward a side exit. "Let's bounce," he says. "This place is about to get too lame. I'm not meant for jail. This horse likes to run free."

"I can't leave my brothers," I say, starting to pull away just as I see Duke. I grab his hand, and we run. We're laughing, but my heart thuds with fear and excitement and danger all rolled into one. My brothers don't let me do this kind of thing, don't include me in it. Baron's with us by the time we hit the door, bursting out into the chilly, damp evening. A haze surrounds the streetlamps, and music thumps faintly from inside the hall. Our footfalls echo across the pavement, along with Dolly's laugh, which is bigger and bawdier than I expected, and Dixie's girlish giggle.

Blue lights bath the parking lot in a silent, incessant pulse like a heartbeat. Devlin leads the way through the parking lot, skidding to a stop when we reach his new red convertible. He hits the top, and it recedes while we all wait, barely able to contain ourselves from leaping in before the top's down. Devlin is already in the front seat, dragging me into his lap. Colt hops over the door into the passenger seat, hauling Dixie over the side of the car into his lap. All I can see are her legs sticking up over a front seat full of satin and tulle, and I start laughing as the car lurches forward.

Colt whoops from under the ocean of Dixie's dress, and Devlin swears and swerves out of the lot, shooting through the night. The cool, damp wind snatches my breath as we streak through the dark streets of Faulkner. The moon hangs like a round, white pumpkin in the sky, millions of stars flung out from it in every direction. I take a deep breath of the fresh air. This is small-town life, but it feels like I'm living bigger than I ever have before.

We wind along two-lane roads through the woods, at last pulling up in a gravel drive that's all too familiar.

"Welcome to the after party," Colt says, spilling out the door with Dixie still in his arms. The twins hop out, each of them holding one of Dolly's hands. So that's how that's going down, then.

"Shit," I say. "We left Royal."

"He can have the limo," Colt says.

"And my date," Baron says. He and Duke crack up, and Devlin leads us up the steps and into his mom's house. It's apparently empty.

Devlin leads us into a small alcove off the kitchen and throws wide the glass doors of a set of cabinets. Expensive bottles of liquor are packed into every inch.

Colt grabs a bottle of tequila and hefts it like a trophy. "Let's get the real party started!"

twenty-three

I wake to the pounding in my own head. I'm cocooned in warmth, and for a minute, I don't want to move. But as consciousness swims up to meet me, I remember the night before. I roll over, only to find myself staring at a horrifyingly bare chest.

"Fuck!" I whisper, sitting up and staring in disbelief. "Fuck fuck fuck."

I'm not wearing anything but a bra and underwear, and something on my stomach feels sticky. I close my eyes and pray it's vomit. I remember getting sick. I remember Devlin feeding me shots until I puked, and then trying to feed me more, but I kept puking until he gave up. What I don't remember is after that. I don't remember leaving the party. I don't remember losing my pants. I don't know how I got here. I don't even know where *here* is.

When I open my eyes, the boy is still there. The beautiful, terrible boy who tormented me on Friday night and came for me on Saturday like a claiming. The boy whose parents didn't even care enough to interrupt when he held me down and held a knife to my face, and the boy who refused to leave a high school dance until he'd had one dance with me. The boy whose arms are wrapped around me like a lover's, whose face looks like an angel with the sun gleaming off his blond strands as they lay rumpled on the pillow.

For one second, I think about letting him sleep. About letting him wake up and think it was a sweet dream or not remember it at all.

But he doesn't deserve that courtesy.

I lean away from him, holding the blankets to my chest, and slap his shoulder. Hard.

"Hey," I bark.

"Ow," Devlin grumbles, moving away from me a little but not opening his eyes.

I shove his shoulder this time. "Wake up."

"What's your problem?" he mumbles, propping himself up on his elbows. As recognition dawns on his face, he pushes himself up to sitting and drops his head into his hands, muttering curses under his breath.

"What's my problem?" I ask, an incredulous laugh bubbling from within me. "Are you fucking serious right now, Devlin? What's your problem? No, don't even answer that. There's not enough time in a day to explain how truly and deeply fucked up you must be to do what you did to me the other night, and then waltz into the dance last night like you wanted me."

He lifts his head and blinks at me as if he thinks I might morph into someone else. "Did we fuck?"

"I don't fucking know," I say, throwing my hands up. "The last thing I remember is taking shots until I blacked out."

But oh god. I remember more than that. It comes back to me in flashes, like photographs of somebody else. Everyone leaping into his car. The ride through town that felt like all of life was in that car. Shots. Dolly sandwiched between the twins. Oh god. Did I give Devlin a lap dance?

"Are you on birth control?" he asks.

Like that's his only concern. Whether he knocked me up. Like it's no big deal as long as I'm on something.

Of course, to him it's probably not. That didn't look like the first time he got hammered and out of control. But to me... To me it's a big fucking deal.

"No," I admit, my eyes searching Devlin's crystal blue gaze. For the first time since I've met him, he looks genuinely concerned. There's no sign of his sadistic smirk or his angry scowl. For a minute, I let myself think we're in this together. That if I'm pregnant, he's going to be part of it.

"Well, can you tell? Does it feel like we did?" He cuts his eyes toward my lap.

"How would I know?"

"Trust me, unless you're loose as a porn star, you'd be able to tell," he says with a smirk. That's when I remember this isn't someone who's going to stand by me if something happens—even his baby. Devlin despises me.

Humiliation and rage burn through me as I slide a hand between my thighs. I press my fingers against my panties. My jaw and neck ache from where he grabbed me on Friday night.

My ribs feel bruises from the crush of his knees when he squeezed me. My thighs are sore from dancing last night, my throat hurts from vomiting, and my head pounds from alcohol. But when I touch myself, it doesn't hurt.

Thank fuck. I close my eyes and melt with a sigh of relief.

Devlin draws a ragged breath, and my eyes snap open. He's staring at me with such intensity that I can see the ache in his eyes. The fire I see there is different from the rage I know, from the intensity last night. It's a flame of pure, incinerating lust.

I suck in a breath, a tremor of fear and anticipation shimmering through me and settling into a delicious pressure in my low belly. Biting down on my lower lip, I shake my head. "No," I whisper. "It doesn't hurt."

Devlin pounces. He's so quick I can't react before he's crouched over me, bracing himself on his fists and knees. "I can make you hurt so good," he breathes against my neck, his lips skimming the sensitive skin of my throat and sending a current of heat rushing through me. He rocks forward, his broad shoulders crowding my narrow ones. His bare, hot skin against mine does something my brain has no control over.

"Devlin, don't," I whisper, but he's already crowded me back until I'm flat on the bed under him. My heart thuds in my chest, and I press my palms flat against him.

"I'm so hard it hurts," he says, his words sending a shot of adrenaline through me, the pulse of it throbbing between my legs. "Let me make you feel this way, too."

"We can't." My resolve is crumbling though, my body warring with what I know, telling me there is more than I've ever imagined. There is a whole world I've never explored, and right now, the only people in that world are me and Devlin Darling. Nothing else exists.

"Just once," he whispers against my ear, his lips soft as they skim the shell of my ear, tugging gently at my earlobe. "We won't tell anyone."

"We hate each other," I remind him.

He chuckles softly, lowering his body slowly toward mine. Every inch of my skin trembles with anticipation, aching to meet his. "Hate sex is the best sex, right, Manhattan?"

A flash of shock goes through me when I feel something hot, and hard, and bare pressing against my thigh. He's naked. Fuck. Devlin's naked. What did we do last night?

289

"I wouldn't know, okay?" I say, shoving at his chest. My palms don't even move him. He's like a solid wall of muscle looming over me. And god, it feels so good. To my horror, my body responds to him, and it's all I can do not to wrap my legs around him, not to run my hands over every inch of his hot, bare skin. He moves his hips between mine, grazing the head of his cock against my panties, then moving his hips forward inch by inch, so the length of his erection slowly grazes against me to the very base.

I gulp at the thought of that thing even beginning to fit inside me.

"You don't like hate sex?" Devlin asks, his lips teasing my skin softly, sending shivers through every inch of me. "I'll make you hurt so good you never forget it."

"I don't know what I like," I admit. "I've never done this."

Devlin lets out a snort of breath. "Sure, Manhattan. You're a tight little virgin. Is that what the boys back home wanted to hear?"

"It's true," I say, blood rushing in my ears. My head knows this is complete insanity, but my body can't help responding to his. When I feel his hardness pulse against my belly, I can barely breathe.

"Okay," Devlin says, his lips skimming my cheek. "I'll play along. I've never done this, either. But I can be gentle." His words are soft but carry an edge of mockery.

"Get off me," I say, shoving at him again.

He laughs softly and nips at my lower lip. He catches it between his teeth and skims his tongue along it, settling his weight onto me fully. "Oh, come on, baby," he croons in that sweet, honey voice. "Let me be the first to fuck you, raw. With nothing between us. Let me rip you open and make you bleed. Let me cum inside that bloody cunt. I'll glue you back together with my cum and send you limping home to your brothers so they can each have a turn."

"What the fuck is wrong with you?" I ask, squirming to free myself. Devlin pins me with his hips, grinding against me. I can feel the wetness between my thighs, and Devlin must feel it, too, because triumph lights in his eyes.

"You like that, don't you?" he asks, moving his hips in a slow circle. "You little slut. You like the dirty talk."

"I don't," I insist, my face heating.

Devlin chuckles again and brushes his lips over mine before cracking a smile. "Liar. You're wet. Let me taste you. I want to lick that sweet, tight cunt."

"Stop," I breathe, but so many sensations are rolling through my body that I don't even know what I want anymore.

"It's okay," he murmurs, his voice silk against my throat. "You can admit it. We've all got our dirty little secrets. Or is it the mention of your brothers that's got you all hot and bothered? Because my family may be fucked up, but that's some sick shit. Do you fuck them? Or just give them a little taste of your Dolce sweets?"

"I mean it. Stop."

"I can't stop now," he says, his lips teasing, tasting, driving me insane. "You got me started."

Shivers run through me at the gentle caress of his lips while the coarse words tumble from them. The animal heat and muscle of his body make me tremble with fear even as I thrill for more.

He settles deeper against me, his lips pressing a real kiss onto mine at last. I nearly melt with relief, desire racing through me and clenching between my thighs as his tongue strokes my lip. A gasp escapes me, and he growls, dipping his tongue between my lips. He tastes my mouth gently, and heat coils through me, fluttering in my lower belly before settling as an ache in my core. Devlin rolls his hips against mine, his tongue sliding deeper, rhythmically stroking mine.

He reaches down, tugging my panties over my hip. I try to protest, but it comes out as a moan into his mouth. He answers with one of his own, and the vibration of his voice through me makes me go weak all over. He pushes my panties down further, burying his hand between my thighs. Dipping a finger into my slit, he wets it before pushing it deep into me.

"Oh fuck," he groans, breaking the kiss and speaking into the hollow of my throat, his voice hoarse and breathless. "You weren't lying, were you?"

I try to snap at him, but my voice comes out as breathy as his. "No, I wasn't lying."

He pushes his finger deeper, pumping it into me a few times. "I'm going to make you come," he says against my throat. "But I can't fuck you if you're a virgin, Crystal. You deserve someone better than me. I'll just fuck you up and leave you all broken."

"Break me."

Now that he's taken it off the table, it's all I want. I tease my lips against his ear, a shudder running through my whole body at the sensation of his body responding. I clutch his shoulders, rocking my hips against his hand, an exquisite pressure building inside me as his finger moves, fluttering against my walls and coiling the tension inside me tighter and tighter. At last, I let go, let myself go to the one pleasure that all the money and luxury in the world can't provide. It's the one thing I've always been forbidden, and I take it now greedily, crying out Devlin's name helplessly as he brings me to this new place of discovery.

twenty-four

"Wow," I whisper when Devlin pulls back. He slides his wet finger into his mouth and closes his eyes, breathing deeply as he draws the finger slowly out.

"One more," he says, scooting down the bed.

I catch his shoulders, my eyes wide. "I haven't showered."

A smile quirks the corner of his mouth. "One taste isn't enough," he says, diving lower and burying his face between my thighs. I tense, squeezing my knees around his head and grabbing his chin, trying to pull him away. He pushes my hands away and slips his tongue between my lips. A wave of pleasure ripples through me, even better than the last one. I gasp, my knees falling open, and Devlin moans into me like I'm the most exquisite dessert, as sweet as my name.

And again, I let myself have this. I let myself feel the stroke of his warm, wet tongue in places I've never been touched or tasted. I let him carry me up and up, until I'm flying, the tension inside me so tight I think I'll snap in two.

"Devlin," I gasp, burying my fingers in his hair.

He lifts his face and slides back up my body, a broad grin on his face. "Yeah?" he asks, leaning down to kiss my lips. I can feel the raw heat of his bare skin pushing against my wet, sensitive flesh, and I know there's only one thing I want. Only one thing will ease the ache inside me.

"Do it," I whisper, my heart hammering in my chest.

"Really?" he asks. "You want me to fuck you?"

"Yes." I slide my arms around him and squeeze myself to him, pressing my heart to his. I can feel the rapid beat of his heart as it races with mine.

"Say it," he says, his blue eyes blazing with lust as he watches my lips.

"What?"

"Tell me to fuck you," he says. "Say please."

"Please," I whisper.

"Please…?"

I swallow hard and search his blue eyes before whispering, "Fuck me."

His hardness throbs against me, and I gasp. He licks his lips, his breath coming fast, and pushes forward. The strain is almost unbearable, an ache as he tries to break into me. With a growl, he gives a sharp thrust and breaches my entrance. I gasp out, but he pushes deeper still.

He stops, his muscles trembling with the effort of restraining himself. I feel a tightness inside me pulling until it threatens to tear apart. I don't know how he's holding back. I want to scream with pleasure and pain at the same time. My nails bite into his shoulders, and I open my knees wide for him.

"Last chance," he whispers, his breath hot against my neck. "Do you really want to give your virginity to a guy you hate?"

"I don't hate you."

"You will later."

"I can't hate you after this."

"You will," he says again. "But not as much as I'll hate myself for this."

"Wait," I say, grabbing his arms. "A condom."

"No," he says, staring down into my eyes. "I want to feel you raw when I rip you open and wreck you."

My whole body trembles, and I know I couldn't stop him if I wanted to. And the truth is, I want to feel him, too. I want to feel his bare skin with nothing between us but this insatiable need. It's as if every moment before this one was a dance leading to this inevitable collision, as if it were all a storm brewing. Tonight, the storm breaks. Tonight, it rages.

"Take it," I say, and he flexes his hips, breaking me open and forcing his full length past the barrier, burying it deep inside me.

I cry out in pain, my whole body clenching. Devlin lets out a choked groan, reaching down and prying my legs open, spreading them wide and grinding himself deeper, until our hips meet. I can feel the hot length of him throbbing inside me, stretching me to bursting, and tears spring to my eyes. Devlin draws back and thrusts into me hard again, ploughing me open to take his size.

I bite down my lip so I won't cry out again, but I can't help it. Pain clutches me in its teeth, and it's all I can do to keep from sobbing. Devlin leans up on his elbows for leverage and drives into me with deep, powerful thrusts. Each one draws a cry from my lips, but after a while, the cries turn from pain to pleasure. Devlin goes even harder, a primal, animal grunt escaping his throat each time he slams into me with bruising force. I want his roughness, need his violence.

"Harder," I gasp, and he hammers into me so hard my head bangs against the headboard, over and over until I can't do anything but hold on to him and let go of everything else in the world.

"I'm gonna cum inside you," he says, his voice rough and wild.

"Devlin—"

"Shut up and come with me," he says, lowering himself onto his elbows.

I wrap my arms around his neck, throw my head back and close my eyes, but Devlin takes my chin in his hand and lowers it. "Open your eyes," he purrs.

SELENA

Our gazes lock together, and he begins to move again, slowly at first and then harder again. The connection between us is so intense I can't bear it, but I can't close my eyes, either. Pleasure builds in my body, and I wrap my legs around him and grind myself up against him. The tension inside me coils tighter and tighter, and Devlin bites down on his lip and grabs my thigh, lifting it higher and driving into me one last time and not pulling back.

My insides feel raw and sore, and a shock of pain goes through me as he stays locked there, forcing me to take every agonizing inch of him. He grinds against me harder, his hips flexing as heat blossoms inside me when he fills me. The sensation of him spilling into me sends a shock of forbidden excitement through me, and despite the pain, my own pleasure crests again. I gasp out his name as orgasm grips me, pulses rippling through my body as he throbs inside me over and over, giving me everything.

Afterwards, Devlin collapses onto me, clutching me to his chest like something precious that he's about to lose. I thread my fingers through his hair, holding him close and cradling his body in mine.

"I'm sorry," he says against the crook of my neck, his voice choked.

"It's okay," I say, laughing a little. "Pretty sure I got more than you did today."

He doesn't answer, and for a long time, neither of us move. Our skin is slicked with sweat, but I only inhale his scent, relishing the salty tang of his skin and the scent of shampoo in his blond strands when I press a kiss to his head.

I'm dozing when a rap sounds on the other side of the wall. Devlin stiffens, but when the knock doesn't sound again, he slides out of me and rolls off the bed. Turning his back, he picks up his jeans from the floor and pulls them on.

"Is everything okay?" I ask, suddenly vulnerable in this big bed alone.

"Yeah," he says, leaning over to give me a quick kiss. "We'd better get up, though."

I swallow hard and nod, a knot forming in my throat. I don't want to get up in front of him, but he stands over me with a delighted grin on his face. "Now you're shy?" he asks, his eyes glinting with humor.

"Well…"

"Crystal," he says. "I just saw every inch of you, and went down on you, and made you cum screaming my name while I came inside you. I think we're past being shy about nudity."

I let out a scoff of frustration. He's a guy—an experienced guy. Of course he wouldn't get it. Gritting my teeth, I throw off the sheet and hop off the bed. There's a big red stain on the white sheet where I lay.

"Fuck," I say. "I'm sorry. I can... Pay for dry cleaning or something."

Devlin bursts out laughing. It's the first time I've ever heard him genuinely laugh, and it's even more startling than his voice. His laugh is low and rich and sweet as his voice, a sound so beautiful it twists painfully in my chest. I simultaneously wish he laughed more and am selfishly glad that I'm one of what must be a small handful of people who see something rare and genuine from Devlin Darling.

"You're the cutest thing I've ever seen," he says, his eyes sparkling with humor.

"Shut up," I say, turning away to hide my embarrassment. I mean, I fucking bled all over a guy's sheets. That's something so humiliating that even hearing his laugh can't erase the embarrassment completely. My homecoming dress lies crumpled on the floor, too sad and pathetic to put on again. That sure as hell won't save my dignity. Ignoring it, I stomp over to his dresser and grab out a T-shirt.

"What are you doing?" Devlin asks.

"Getting dressed," I say, pulling it over my head. "I'm not wearing my dress and doing the walk of shame. Fuck that."

Before he can answer, I turn and yank open another drawer, finding a pair of sweatpants. They're ridiculously long and baggy on me, but I tie the drawstring and make do.

When I turn back to Devlin, a small smile plays over his lips, his expression infuriatingly unreadable.

"What?" I ask.

"Nothing," he says. "That's weirdly hot."

I grab my shoes off the floor and stuff my feet into them, ignoring Devlin's snickers. When I look up, though, he's not laughing at me, not in the mean way he has before.

"Come 'ere," he says, slinging an arm around me and pulling me in, pressing his lips to my forehead. I resist for a moment, but all I want to do is pull him back onto the bed, curl up in his arms, and stay there forever. I rest my hands on his hips, closing my eyes and breathing him in as deeply as I can, as if I can save this moment forever.

"What now?" I whisper, not daring to open my eyes.

"Shhh," Devlin says, resting his cheek against the top of my head.

A minute later, knuckles rap on the door, and Devlin pulls away. Without a word, he turns and walks out into the hall. Taking a deep breath, I follow.

To our left, the twins stand with Dolly between them. She's wearing full, fresh makeup and her dress from the night before, which looks as fresh as if she hung it in the closet overnight, but her expression is wary as she watches us as if waiting for some judgment.

Devlin's judgment, I realize. I look to him, but I can't read his expression. He gives them a cool look before turning to the other side. Colt is standing in the hall, having just knocked. Dixie stands behind him wearing her rumpled homecoming dress and holding her shoes in her hand. Her lipstick is gone, and her eye makeup is smudged. Her face is pale under her freckles, and for once, I can't read her expression. She's just... Blank.

Footsteps sound on the stairs, and Preston appears looking freshly showered and shaved, his short hair spiked up and a feverish excitement lighting his eyes. He stops when he reaches the landing, and his gaze skims over all of us in one sweep. A shit-eating grin spreads across his face as he stands there waiting, a hand on the railing.

Devlin looks back and forth between us all, and something snaps down over his eyes as if he's just put on a mask. I can almost feel the temperature drop around him. The playful, dirty-talking, lustful Devlin is gone, replaced with the cold, cruel boy I've walked the halls with at school.

"Did you nail 'em?" Preston asks.

"Yeah," Colt says with a grin, turning to Devlin. "Did you?"

"Yeah," Devlin says. "Sometimes you gotta throw a dog a bone."

Colt's smile grows wider, and he leers at me in Devlin's oversized clothes, so casually callous that it makes me want to wrap my arms around myself and hide. His gaze that makes me feel like a commodity whose value he's appraising. He holds up a hand for Devlin to high-five, but Devlin turns on his heel, facing my brothers. "Get out of my house," he says. "And take your whores with you."

"So I guess that truce was just... What?" I ask, too stung to put up any pretense of cool. "A ploy to get in my pants?"

"Oh, sweetheart," Devlin says. "Don't be naïve. This was never about you."

"Liar," I whisper, staring up at him like he's a stranger. He is. The boy in that room is not the same boy who stands here, not even looking at me.

Colt grins, the smile that never reaches his eyes. "Why don't you run to daddy and have him fly you back to New York where you belong?"

"You," I hiss, my words laced with poison. "You're a liar, too."

"Did you really think you could be on the same level as the Darlings?" he asks, giving me a pitying look.

"Our family has a name, a history of wealth and privilege," Devlin says, looking past me to Duke. "We're this town's royalty. You think you're rich, that you can compete with the likes of us? You're just poor white trash playing dress-up."

Colt pushes Dixie toward me, barely sparing her a glance. He's speaking to me. To our family. "Go back to where you came from. You'll never belong in this town, and you'll never belong among the likes of the Darlings."

Duke springs forward, but I dart between them, pressing my palm against his chest. "Let's just go," I say, keeping my voice low and steady. I turn back to Dixie. "Come on."

She gives one pathetic, hopeful look at Colt that nearly breaks my heart. But I have to keep it together right now before someone gets murdered. And I know that's what'll happen if I let go of my control, because I'm the one who would do the killing.

Preston steps up behind the twins and takes Dolly's elbow. "Beautiful job," he says, smiling at her. "You provided quite the distraction, didn't you, little minx?"

"Dolly's with us now," Baron says, wrapping an arm around her waist from behind.

I stop, glancing between this girl who was apparently part of some elaborate plan to destroy us, and my brothers, who seemingly still want her.

For a second, no one speaks. Then Dolly pulls herself up to her full, impressive height. "I've had enough of being the Darling's pawn," she says, staring straight at Devlin.

A flicker of surprise crosses his face, along with something else I can't identify before it's gone. This girl isn't just Devlin's fangirl. She's someone so important to him that all his fangirls carry her stamp. Someone he's known all his life, who might be his first love, his first kiss, his first time.

The thought makes something funny turn over inside me.

"What are you saying, Dolly?" Devlin asks. "You're not a pawn."

"Aren't I?" she asks, a challenge in her voice. She turns from him to Colt, and lastly to Preston, who still stands against the railing of the upstairs balcony. "You might say otherwise, but this girl opened my eyes."

When she looks at me, all the Darlings do, too. A week ago, a day ago, I would have cringed. But what are they going to do to me now? They had me. They broke me. There's nothing left to fear.

Dolly's on a roll, and she keeps going. She's a sight to behold, well over six feet with her hair piled as high as it is and her six-inch heels. "The only difference between a Darling Doll and a Darling Dog is that you say there is a difference," she says. "In truth, we're all the same. We all do your bidding. But you know what? I'm not a doll. I'm tired of acting like one, waiting for you to take me down and play with me."

"Aw, baby, we're not playing with you," Colt says.

"I'm done," she says, glaring at Devlin. "With you, with your cousins, with all of you."

If she's trying to get him to flinch, she's in for some sobering truth. He doesn't even blink, just stares back at her, his eyes cold as a snake's, unaffected by her words.

"Then let's go," I say. "We're all done here."

Devlin stares at my brothers, not even bothering to glance at me as I walk away. I can't feel my legs, only an ache between them reminding me that Devlin took something from me I'll never get back. I keep waiting for his words to come true, for me to start hating him. But I don't. I can't feel anything but a coldness where my heart should be. This must be how Devlin feels all the time. Heartless. Emotionless. Ruthless.

I run my fingers along the banister all the way down the winding staircase, trying to feel some kind of nostalgia for the place where I lost my virginity. Each step makes a dart of pain shoot between my legs, but I don't walk carefully. I relish the pain. The dirty, wet feeling of Devlin's cum still trickling out of me, wetting my underwear. I don't look back, but I hear the footsteps of my brothers on the stairs. The clack of Dolly's heels, and the muffled thud of Dixie's bare footfalls join them. I can't hear my own feet, can't feel them. It's as if I'm floating.

I don't stop until I reach the gravel drive. That's when reality hits. We're here without a car. Dolly groans and rubs her forehead, squinting against the bright, late-morning sun. Dixie hasn't said a word. Someone shut her up at last. She stands there like a shell-shocked ghost.

"I'll call King," Baron says, taking out his phone.

"Did you really fuck Devlin Darling?" Duke asks, staring at me. I understand everything in that look. Like he's not sure he can keep it together, like he might explode at any moment.

Like he doesn't know who I am anymore, like he can't make sense of a world where I've done the thing I've done. Like he's not sure if he still loves and respects me, or if he's ashamed to call me his sister. I understand everything in his eyes as if they're a mirror to my own feelings about myself.

"Does it really matter?" I ask.

Baron hangs up his phone and turns to us, his face pale and sober. Dread twists hard in my chest, and for a second, I can't breathe.

"Royal," I whisper.

"King's coming to get us," he says, staring at the house behind me.

"What's wrong?"

Baron forces his gaze to mine. "He never made it home last night."

"Maybe he went home with someone," I say, my voice thin with panic.

Royal is the only one of my brothers who isn't like that. He doesn't just go home with girls.

"King already talked to the limo driver," Baron says. "Royal left right after us, and the driver dropped him off at the end of the driveway."

"What?" I ask, barely able to breathe past the knot in my throat.

Baron glances at the house where the Darling cousins remain, his jaw hard. "The driver said Royal met a man in the driveway. He didn't see much because it was dark, but he described the guy as tall and blond."

"Preston," I whisper. Was that all this was? A decoy? A distraction?

"The driver left when they were just talking," Baron says. "But King says Royal never made it to the house."

"You don't think…" I break off and swallow hard, not finishing that sentence. I don't have to. We're all thinking the same thing. Devlin said it wasn't personal, but he has no idea what he's dealing with. We're the Dolces, and we're anything but sweet. Our blood is thicker than chocolate. Our family always comes first. And if they hurt our family, things are about to get really fucking personal. Because if they hurt my brothers, I'll hunt them to the ends of the earth to exact revenge.

Printed in Great Britain
by Amazon

19305006R00185